P9-CCR-056

THE GADGET

BOOKS BY PAUL ZINDEL

The Pigman
Outstanding Children's Books of 1968, *The New York Times*
Notable Children's Books, 1940–1970 (ALA)
Best of the Best for Young Adults, 1966–1992 (ALA)
Best Children's Books of 1968 *(Book World)*
1969 Fanfare Honor List *(The Horn Book)*

My Darling, My Hamburger
Outstanding Children's Books of 1969, *The New York Times*

I Never Loved Your Mind
Outstanding Children's Books of 1970, *The New York Times*

The Effect of Gamma Rays on Man-in-the-Moon Marigolds
1971 Pulitzer Prize for Drama
Best American Play of 1970 (New York Drama Desk Critics Circle Award)
Notable Books, 1971 (ALA)
Best of the Best for Young Adults 1966–1988 (ALA)

Pardon Me, You're Stepping on My Eyeball!
Outstanding Children's Books of 1976, *The New York Times*
Best Books for Young Adults, 1976 (ALA)

Confessions of a Teenage Baboon
Best Books for Young Adults, 1977 (ALA)

The Undertaker's Gone Bananas

The Pigman's Legacy
Outstanding Children's Books of 1980, *The New York Times*
Best Books for Young Adults, 1980 (ALA)

A Star for the Latecomer *(with Bonnie Zindel)*

The Girl Who Wanted a Boy

Harry and Hortense at Hormone High

To Take a Dare *(with Crescent Dragonwagon)*
Best Books for Young Adults, 1982 (ALA)

The Amazing and Death-Defying Diary of
Eugene Dingman
(A Charlotte Zolotow Book)
1988 Books for the Teen Age (New York Public Library)

A Begonia for Miss Applebaum
(A Charlotte Zolotow Book)
Best Books for Young Adults, 1989 (ALA)
1990 Books for the Teen Age (New York Public Library)

The Pigman & Me
(A Charlotte Zolotow Book)
Best Books for Young Adults, 1993 (ALA)
Notable Children's Books, 1993 (ALA)
Best Books of 1992 *(School Library Journal)*
1993 Books for the Teen Age (New York Public Library)
Children's Books of 1992 (Library of Congress)
1992 Notable Children's Trade Books in Social Studies (NCSS/CBC)
1993 Fanfare Honor List *(The Horn Book)*
Bulletin Blue Ribbons *(Bulletin of the Center for Children's Books)*

David & Della
(A Charlotte Zolotow Book)
1994 Books for the Teen Age (New York Public Library)

Loch
1995 Recommended Books for the Reluctant Young Adult Reader (ALA)
1995 Books for the Teen Age (New York Public Library)

The Doom Stone
1996 Recommended Books for the Reluctant Young Adult Reader (ALA)
1996 Books for the Teen Age (New York Public Library)

Reef of Death
1999 ALA Quick Picks for Reluctant Young Adult Readers
Children's Choices for 1999 (IRA/CBC)
1999 Books for the Teen Age (New York Public Library)

PAUL ZINDEL

THE GADGET

HARPERCOLLINS*PUBLISHERS*

I wish to thank Professor Richard F. Cahill for his research and
preparation of the appendices; Hiroshi Kanda for sharing his thoughts
and memories of his family; and Lou Chris, who provided me with an
adobe house to live in for six weeks at Ranchos de Taos, New Mexico

The Gadget
Copyright © 2001 by Paul Zindel

Library of Congress Cataloging-in-Publication Data
Zindel, Paul.
    The gadget / by Paul Zindel.
        p.   cm.
    Summary: In 1945, having joined his father at Los Alamos, where he and other scientists
are working on a secret project to end World War II, thirteen-year-old Stephen becomes
caught in a web of secrecy and intrigue.
    ISBN 0-06-027812-9 — ISBN 0-06-028255-X (lib. bdg.)
    1. Manhattan Project (U.S.)—Juvenile fiction.   [1. Manhattan Project (U.S.)—Fiction.
2. Atomic bomb—Fiction.   3. Los Alamos (N.M.)—Fiction.   4. Spies—Fiction.
5. World War, 1939–1945—United States—Fiction.]   I. Title.
PZ7.Z647 Gad   2001   00-38903
[Fic]—dc21   CIP
                                                                              AC

Typography by Al Cetta
1   2   3   4   5   6   7   8   9   10
❖
First Edition

To my sister, Betty,

and her sixty Japanese students

London
October 16, 1944

Stephen waited until his mother and aunt were out in the kitchen making coffee before he slipped away from the family dinner table. He grabbed the binoculars from the sideboard. His cousin Jackson got the crystal radio set out of the hall closet, and the two boys headed for the door.

"Snoopy bruthas!" Jackson's four-year-old sister, Molly, yelled out, pointing at them. "Snoopy bruthas!"

Everyone knew she was trying to say Stephen and Jackson were nosey—and looked like *brothers*—and it was true. Both were gangly with thick, brown hair and squared, sturdy chins.

Stephen certainly had been an inquisitive kid ever since he could crawl. One Christmas he was taken to Macy's department store, and he asked the Santa Claus if he used 5 Day deodorant pads. Another time he had a one-eyed baby-sitter and used to pretend to fall asleep so he could watch her take out her glass eye and put it in a case for the night. And Jackson had never been a slouch in the curiosity department either. He'd never left a door closed nor anyone's package unopened.

The boys were halfway out the door when Stephen's mother came back and spotted them.

"Be careful," she said. "If you hear the air-raid sirens, you both get back down here *straight away.*"

"Right, Mom," Stephen said.

Molly laughed and ran to her phonograph. She started winding it up so she could sway and sing to "G.I. Jive" until she drove everyone crazy.

Jackson led the way up the stairs of the apartment house two at a time. They heard the sounds of other families behind the closed doors: the clinking of dishes being washed and stacked; Mr. Erikson playing scales on his piano; near the sixth floor the smell of shepherd's pie and baking apples. The Rohr twins were getting tangled up in a leash as they came down the stairs with their new spaniel puppy.

Above the top floor Jackson pushed open the heavy metal door to the roof. He and Stephen scooted to their favorite niche in the shadow of a squat, rusting water tank. Every night since Stephen and his mother had arrived in London, Jackson and he had made it a ritual to sit beneath the stars or watch the fog creep in from the Thames.

"I wish it was summer and we were horse-back riding or catching salamanders again," Stephen said.

"Me too. Kirkby River was the best," Jackson said. "The turtles. And the rope swing."

"Remember the leeches? The ones on your back and your horse's legs!"

"You're going to make me throw up," Jackson said.

The boys laughed as they set up their home-made crystal radio—a small coil with magnets and wires mounted in the bottom of a shoe box. Stephen dragged the end of a sharpened wire over the surface of the quartz. There was static, then the faint voice of a woman singing.

"Let's see if we can get Portugal again," Stephen said, moving the wire toward the center of the crystal.

"Or Amsterdam."

The radio voices faded in and out.

"I think I hear German," Jackson said. "That's what it sounds like."

Stephen strained to hear. He was still trying to make out the voice when there came another sound he did recognize. But it wasn't coming from the radio. He felt his stomach tighten.

"Airplanes," he said, looking to the night sky. "Where are they?"

Jackson got to his feet. "I don't know," he said.

Warning sirens began to shriek.

"We'd better go back down," Stephen said. "They're going to want to get us to the shelter."

Jackson pointed toward the horizon. "Look,

here they come." He grabbed the binoculars and looked through them. "It could be our planes. R.A.F. coming back from a raid."

There was a distant flash of light and the high arc of antiaircraft fire. "No. It's Luftwaffe. German planes. They're bombing," Jackson shouted. "Come on." He turned and ran back across the soft tar of the roof and its grid of drainpipes. Stephen followed on his cousin's heels to the roof door. Jackson began banging on the thick sheet of steel.

"What's the matter?" Stephen said.

"It's locked. We forgot to prop it open."

"Let me try."

Stephen was twelve, a year and a half older than Jackson. He was stronger, and he put his shoulder next to Jackson's. Together they grunted, strained to force open the door. It wouldn't budge. Jackson grabbed a piece of jagged loose pipe and tried to wedge it like a crowbar between the door and its frame. The racket of planes and bombing was nearer.

BAM.

A single bomb exploded. The sky around

them began to glow—splashes of yellow and purple mixed with thick curls of black smoke and the shouts of frightened people on the street. The boys frantically kicked the door, trying to jolt it off its hinges.

BAM.

Another bomb. Nearer.

There was sudden fear in Jackson's eyes. He looked dazed now. Confused. Stephen pulled him down to huddle between an air duct and the low, tiled roof wall. We'll be safe here, Stephen thought. The bombing will stop and there'll be the all-clear siren and . . .

Now the bombs fell in clusters, so near they could hear them whistling down before the roof-shuddering blasts. Then there was another high-pitched noise, the mounting scream of a falling rocket bomb. Jackson jumped up, terrified. He had seen what a V-2 could do.

Stephen grabbed his arm.

"Jackson! Stay down."

His cousin clapped his hands over his ears, shook free of Stephen's hand, and ran from the shriek.

"No!" Stephen yelled. "Come back."

The noise was deafening. The rocket bomb hit on the left, and the entire building shook violently. Stephen was stunned by a rippling flash. Half a block of buildings and the front of the church next door disintegrated in an explosion. Tongues of fire and brick and shards of steel shot out from the huge fireball. Nuns and children screamed, fleeing from under the rear buttresses of the collapsing church.

Stephen heard Jackson cry out. He turned and stared helplessly into Jackson's eyes as the corner of the roof crumbled and dropped away.

"No."

Jackson fell backward.

Down.

A wall of heat hit Stephen as he ran to the edge. There were three more explosions. Painful, stinging flashes of light.

When it was over, when the planes had gone, a night wind began to clear the smoke and dust. Stephen started to shiver. Below in the church graveyard he could see Jackson's body—twisted and dead like a torn, bleeding doll.

New Mexico
February 23, 1945
Five Months to Deadline

Stephen had felt on edge from the moment the train raced out of the tunnel north of Santa Fe. It was being cooped up day after day for over two weeks that had made the sinking feeling come back.

The Sangre de Cristo Mountains glowed bloodred in the dawn. From the train window he had watched the snow-dusted peaks and crags give way to rolling hills of ponderosa and cottonwood. Soon the clacking and straining of the train faded as the tracks leveled out across the desert plateau.

On the ship back from England, the returning soldiers had yelped and arm wrestled. They had yakked about what had happened to the Brooklyn Dodgers and who was this month's favorite pinup girl. What about Betty Grable's legs? How do you like that Rita Hayworth?

But on this train ride through New Mexico the new recruits were quiet. They chain-smoked and played seven-card stud. There was no joking. Military police patrolled the aisles. Everything was tense and serious and strained.

Stephen held his dad's last letter. He'd read and reread it on the journey. *There's all kinds of shortages,* his father had written. *Toilet paper. Glue. The spring snow is melting and washing out half the roads. Sometimes the drinking water has worms in it. . . .*

BLACK BLACK BLACK.

The censor's ink had slashed out paragraphs. Pages.

The train braked to a stop at the small station in Lamy. A leathery voice blared from huge speakers atop a mud-covered army van: "All Site Y soldiers and civilians board the busses immediately." A detail of auxiliary M.P.s got on the train and began to sweep through it as if the train were crossing into a foreign country.

Stephen snatched up his pea jacket and suitcase and got off into the chill of the morning air. He figured the handful of nonmilitary men in coats and crushed suits who got off with him were scientists like his father. Other men in scarfs and jackets would be machinists and technicians. Stephen had gotten to recognize the types when his father had been assigned to a secret project at the University of Chicago.

"The U.S. Government welcomes you to New Mexico," a nearby M.P. shouted. Stephen looked around for his father. There were no familiar faces.

Stephen climbed into the last of the busses in the convoy. The driver shifted, and the muscled slab of an M.P. stood next to him, roaring to be heard above the growling engine. "We'll be traveling thirty-five miles northwest of Santa Fe to a mesa. Mesa means table around these parts. You're going to be living at seven thousand feet above sea level, so you may have difficulty breathing. Don't worry about it. You'll get used to it.

"You can now know our destination is officially identified as *Los Alamos*. It is not on any map. It is classified. Anything about it—anything!—is not to pass your lips. There are spies on base and off. There are saboteurs. You are to trust no one."

Rain began to fall in drenching sheets, hammering the clay-tiled roofs and early-morning streets of Santa Fe. Stephen reached up to his neck to check for the shiny flattened sixpence. A few weeks before, when safe ocean passage from England had opened up for him, his mother had had the coin pressed and stamped by a souvenir machine at an arcade. *REMEMBER US* was the message she had picked out. Then she'd had the coin strung on a thin silver chain.

"Thirteen is a very important birthday," she had said as she hung the coin around his neck. "I'm sorry I couldn't have gotten you a bike or the chemistry set you wanted. When the war's over, I'll buy you a proper gift. We'll have a home in the States. You, me, and your father. We'll be together and our lives will be ordinary again."

Stephen straddled his suitcase with his long legs and held tight as the bus drove through the main square. Soon the convoy turned north onto a main highway and climbed a steep slope. The roadway descended briefly into a forest, then rose again into a maze of turns and a rutted single-lane road. As the bus crossed over a deep gorge, Stephen had to close his eyes until the bus was on the other side. He hated heights. There was another bolt of lightning. And another closer yet. He thought of his mother again. His mother and all the family who were refusing to flee from London during the German bomb raids. His aunts and uncles, and his grandmother in Coventry . . .

Why couldn't you have at least come and met me, Dad? Why couldn't you?

"Los Alamos straight ahead," the M.P. shouted, pulling Stephen out of his memory and back to the overcrowded troop bus. "I.D.s ready. Have your I.D.s ready."

The entire perimeter of the base was surrounded by a high double fence. As the convoy passed through the gate of the main entrance, Stephen noticed a big redheaded man letting a dozen German shepherds out of a van. A sun-wrinkled woman in a long skirt helped load other dogs into a long truck with a caged bed.

A changing of the guard dogs.

M.P.s halted the busses and ordered everyone off.

"Civilians to the left, Army personnel to the right," the ranking M.P. shouted. Stephen went left and showed his passport. He glanced around. Still there was no sign of his father.

"Wait for your escorts," another M.P. ordered, herding the new arrivals into a maze of chain-link fencing. Stephen looked beyond the barrier to the base itself, a cluster of low and flat clapboard buildings, all painted green. There were no trees on the base. Instead, hundreds of telephone poles rose from the compound. *I'm going to live in a town with a fence around it. A town completely fenced.*

"Stephen," called a rough, deep voice.

An Indian woman walked toward him. She looked to be about thirty years old, stubby and solid, with broad shoulders like a man. A pair of alert, dark eyes stared at him from under a purple shawl she wore like a hood.

"Your father couldn't get away from the lab," the woman said.

"How come?"

The woman looked surprised at his question. "I didn't ask," she said. "Come. I'm Sewa, your dad's housekeeper. He told me to get you. "

She smiled and shook his hand.

"When can I see him?" Stephen asked.

"You're having dinner with him tonight at the dining hall," Sewa said. "Good food. It's stuffed-pork-chop night—all you can eat—and applesauce."

She led the way out of the holding pen and down a dirt road lined with shacks, Sundt houses, and metal Quonset huts. Narrow walkways were laid out across stretches of ice and mud, like lines on a chessboard. Sewa had to shout above the clamor of heavy digging machines. "They're building more houses. There are many more soldiers and scientists coming. They need buildings to live in. But you are lucky. You will be very comfortable in Bathtub Row."

Stephen hurried to keep up with her. "What is *that*?"

"The place where you live," Sewa said. "Bathtub Row is the street with the best houses. Not junky houses. Your father is a V.I.P., so he got a deluxe log house. One with a bathtub. There are only nine bathtubs on the base. Everyone else has a shower."

Stephen noticed a group of men in lab coats

walking down the street. He recognized a few of the faces from the Army project in Chicago. The scientists went inside a building that had a second barbed-wire fence around it. He knew it must be the Tech Area. Laboratories. Probably the lab where his father worked.

"The Oppenheimers have a bathtub too," Sewa said. "They live next door to your father. We are to call everyone here by code names, but I keep forgetting them. I came to work here when they first built the base. The secrecy drove me crazy at first."

"Are there really saboteurs and kidnappers?"

"Sure. Why not?"

"Did anything ever happen? Was anyone ever kidnapped?"

"Not that I know of. The Army must think nobody's one-hundred-percent safe. They don't want anyone to know anything. The streets have no names. This is a town that doesn't exist. They want everyone to say they live at P.O. Box 1663 in Santa Fe."

Stephen followed Sewa up the walk toward a sprawling stone-and-log ranch house. Inside, the rooms were damp and cold. There was the smell of cedar as she led him through the dark living room and down a narrow hallway.

"This is your room," Sewa said, stopping at the first doorway. "Watch out for ticks the size of quarters."

"You're kidding."

"Nope."

Stephen hesitated, then went in. The windows of the room had heavy shutters. A single bed was covered by a shaggy blanket woven with designs of thunderbolts and snakes. Stephen put down his suitcase and opened the shutters.

"The post exchange has Devil Dogs and Flako piecrust mix. There are many privileges and luxuries for the scientists and their families. Would you like a toasted cheese sandwich?"

"I don't think so."

"A Tootsie Roll?"

"No, thanks."

Stephen sat down on the bed. The mattress was lumpy. "I'm tired. The days on the train were worse than the week crossing the Atlantic."

"Why don't you take a nap?"

"I could use one."

"I'll wake you in plenty of time," Sewa said. She started out, but stopped at the doorway and looked back at him as he laid his head down on the pillows. "Dream of magic dogs."

"What?"

"Magic dogs are what my grandfather called horses. To dream of them is to have good luck and find many new friends."

She closed the door behind her.

For a while Stephen listened to the silence of the room. He pulled the Indian blanket up around him. The cases on the pillows were clean but frayed. They smelled of a strong soap. He reached his hand up to the sixpence that was hanging around his neck. He could feel the stamped letters of *REMEMBER US*.

When Stephen awoke, it was dark. He rushed out of his room, nearly running into Sewa. She was wearing an apron and carrying a tray.

"Whoa," she said. "Don't worry—your father called from the lab. He said you can meet him at seven thirty. He said he was running late."

"Oh . . ."

"I baked corn crisps and made you a glass of chocolate milk."

"Thanks."

Stephen took the tray of snacks into his room and unpacked his shirts and underwear from his suitcase. He had arranged everything so it would protect his collection of airplane models and a journal crammed full of scribblings and newspaper clippings. He used tacks to hang his balsa-wood planes from a beam above a desk in the corner, and put away his journal.

"I'm heading over to the dining room," he told Sewa when he was finished. "I don't like waiting for stuff."

"I understand," Sewa said, reaching into the pocket of her apron. She took out a small metal badge with a number on it and a safety pin soldered to its back. "This is your I.D. You're expected to wear it whenever you go out. We use numbers, not names."

"I had to wear one in Chicago."

"Good—then you won't forget to do the same

thing here," she said, pinning it to his coat lapel. She walked him outside and pointed down the street. "Straight ahead and you'll see the dining room. It looks like a big old roller-skating rink. Make sure you—"

"I know," Stephen said. "I'll watch out for spies and saboteurs."

"You'll be safe on the base, but if you see any-thing strange—or if something bothers you—go with your instincts and report it to one of the Military Police." She called across the dirt street to the M.P. patrolling Bathtub Row. "Mitchell, this is Stephen—Dr. Orr's son. He's staying with us now."

The M.P., a barrel-chested young man with a crew cut, gave a polite salute.

Stephen gave him a wave and started down the street. There were uniformed staff and military personnel in fatigues on the main walkways, men and women moving at a good clip. Jeeps and vans drove by, their tires breaking the layers of forming ice and kicking up the soft mud beneath. There were some familiar faces. He nodded to a physicist he recognized from the

Chicago project. The man acted as if he didn't see him or just couldn't bother to say hello.

Stephen walked along the perimeter fence. Dusk was creeping over the Jemez Mountains to the west. Several guard dogs, their tails wagging, trailed him along the chain-link barrier. He knew if he trespassed into their territory, they'd grab his arms in their teeth and pin him down in a flash.

There was a towering fence around the Tech Area. It was topped with rolls of barbed wire, and a half dozen M.P.s were checking the badges of everyone going in or out.

Soon he arrived at the long, flat rectangle that was the base dining hall, and he went in.

"Can I help you?" the hostess asked.

She smelled of roses. Her jet-black hair was immaculately parted and pulled back close to her head. He knew she probably was a wife of one of the chemists or physicists. His father had written that all the wives on base had to work. The only other women around were the Indian housekeepers and a regiment of WACs.

"I'm supposed to meet my father," Stephen

said. He lowered his voice. "Dr. Orr. I don't know his code name yet."

"Oh, you're *Stephen*."

"Yes."

"He told me to keep an eye out for you," the hostess said. "You look like your dad."

"Thanks."

She led the way to one of the tables set off by a row of rubber plants and palms. He sat down and spotted his father—white lab coat, his head at a pompous tilt—coming into the dining room. Walking with him was a graying, stern man wearing the cap and uniform of a general. The general's paunch spilled out over his regulation canvas U.S. Army belt.

Dr. Orr peeled away from the general.

Stephen was on his feet.

A year, Dad, since Mom and I went to London. A year we've been without you. . . .

"Hi, son," Dr. Orr said. He reached out to shake his son's hand.

For a moment Stephen looked at the hand like it belonged to a stranger. He surprised himself when he realized he wanted to hit this man. Punch him. He wanted to hurt his own dad. Instead, he grasped his father's hand and shook it.

"Long time no see," Stephen said.

Stephen fought to hide his anger. It had rushed up from corners he hadn't known were inside him. *You haven't seen me in a year and all you do is shake my hand? If you hadn't accepted this job in this crazy town, Dad, if you had stayed and helped get the family out of London . . .*

After a moment Stephen had control of himself again. "Why couldn't you at least have met me at the gate?"

"There was something important, an experiment being prepared in the lab," his father said.

"Yes . . ."

They sat down at the table. "Stephen, I knew that Sewa and the M.P.s would look out for you."

Stephen could see his father was thinner than he'd ever seen him. His eyes were swollen, and his hair looked like it needed to be washed. His father's attention drifted to the table where the general and a handful of other scientists sat.

"Mom's gotten Aunt Bea and Grandpa up to the Lake District," Stephen said. "Some of the other relatives are holding out. Mom said to tell you she's trying to finish everything up."

"I've been worried about you and Mom, Stephen. I should have taken you both with me when I left. I know that now. It must have been terrible for you—"

"I'm fine," Stephen said quickly.

His father wasn't looking at him. His mind was elsewhere.

Somewhere.

"Those two guys are my bosses," his father said. "The tall edgy fellow in the suit is Robert Oppenheimer, the top dog here. He calls the shots on all the physics. The science. He's usually got a porkpie hat glued to his head."

"Who's the general?"

"Groves, head of the whole operation. Oppie takes orders from him. They're always at each other's throats."

An Indian girl set bowls of mixed greens in front of them. Stephen ate the shredded carrots and beets from the top and followed his father's gaze back to Oppenheimer. He was even thinner than his father, skeletal, with a sharp nose and receding chin. His arms and hands flew recklessly in the air, punctuating everything.

"The top brains are here," his father said. "There's a whole team from England. Fermi's from Italy. He's sitting to Oppie's right. A Nobel Prize in Physics."

"I've clipped plenty of articles on him."

"Fermi is called 'Mr. Farmer.'"

"I know—code names."

"We call Oppie 'Choirboy' because he grins and acts like a kid a lot of the time. A lot of enthusiasm."

"What's your name?"

"'Olaf.'"

"You're kidding. That means I'm Olaf's son," Stephen complained. "It sounds like I'm the village idiot."

"No, it doesn't."

"Hey, how am I going to remember who's who?"

"It gets easy."

The server set down platters of chops and steamed vegetables, family style, along with a basket of toasted raisin bread. His father's hand shook as he cut the meat.

Suddenly:

CLANG. CLANG. CLANG.

An alarm.

Groves, Oppenheimer, and several of the scientists rushed for the door.

"What's happening?" Stephen asked.

"I'm sorry, Stephen," his father said. He stood up and threw his napkin down on the table. "I'll meet you back at the house." As he left, the clanging stopped and colored lights flashed. An emergency code, a system like they had on the Chicago project.

Outside, Stephen watched M.P.s and soldiers

get into jeeps and vans. Tires spun in the crust of the freezing mud.

An Army ambulance sped by. No siren, only a dome on its roof flashing red. It halted in front of the high-security Tech Area, where several men wearing silver coveralls and carrying glistening instruments rushed out. Dr. Orr and Oppenheimer walked quickly toward a rolling gurney that held a man half wrapped in an aluminum body bag. The man was shaking.

Orr and Oppenheimer kept firing questions at him as he was loaded into the ambulance. Stephen's father and Oppenheimer commandeered a jeep and followed. Something bad had happened. Very bad. For a moment Stephen believed he was back in London. He was on the roof again, and there were bombs falling. . . .

He was with Jackson and the war again.

He hurried back to Bathtub Row. Sewa had left for the night, back to the San Ildefonso Pueblo down the hill. Mitchell let him in. Yes, the M.P. told Stephen, he had heard there was an accident, but he didn't know what it was.

Stephen put on the lights in the house and walked through the chilly rooms. He went into the bathroom and filled up the tub. Soaking in hot water, he felt the cold finally drain from his body. *I shouldn't have come. I should have stayed in England,* he thought.

Why did he even want me here?

When Stephen finally got out of the tub, he dried himself with a coarse, brown towel. He put on his pajamas and climbed into bed. The plate of corn crisps was on the bed stand, and he took a bite of one of the crisps—but it tasted like ashes.

When his father came home, he went to Stephen's room.

"What's going on, Dad? What happened?"

His father sat at the bottom of his bed. "You know I can't tell you that."

"It's that same thing you were working on before, isn't it? The project in Chicago. It's something to do with radioactivity." For the first time since he'd arrived, Stephen had his father's full attention.

"It's something to stop Hitler," his father said, quietly, stretching out.

"Something dangerous," Stephen said. "What happened to the man from the lab could happen to you."

His father signaled Stephen to keep his voice down. "Stephen, we're working on something that could win the war. Something that could stop the Germans and the Japanese in their tracks."

"What is it?"

"You don't have to know. Everyone on base has family, sons, and daughters in the military. Loved ones in danger. That's why the lights burn all night in the Tech Area."

"I know you're busy and that your job's really important. Why'd you send for me?"

"I wanted you here," he said. "I need my family with me. That was the deal. Oppenheimer knew the only way he'd get top men to stay is if we could have our families with us. I've been worried about you and your mom."

"Look at you, Dad. You're—"

"Oppenheimer's pushing himself, too."

"Is it a new fuel you're working on? That's what everyone in Chicago thought when you worked there."

His father sat up on the edge of the bed and put his hand on Stephen's shoulder. "Son, I've never lied to you. The physics of what we're after is new. Untested. Even I get frightened. We're not really sure of what we're doing. We have accidents because we don't quite know how to do what we need to do."

"What could be so important?"

"All I can tell you is that it's a race, Stephen. If we win it before Hitler, if we complete our project here before the Germans or the Japanese do anything like it, we'll win the war."

"And if we don't?"

His father pulled his feet up onto the bed. "If we don't—it's the end of our world as we know it." Slowly his eyes closed. His hand slipped from Stephen's shoulder as he curled himself up like a child. For a long while Stephen lay still and listened to the sounds of his father sleeping. He remembered his father taking him for walks on the beach. Stephen had always found bigger and more exotic seashells than any other kid—shells he later realized his father had bought from a store and tossed so he could find them.

Stephen got out of bed and took a blanket

down from the closet. He pulled it over his father and put out the lights. He decided to forget the accident for a while. Forget the big secret and the race.

Forget that he was born to poke and pry.

Stephen ran his fingers over the coin at his neck. He decided to dream it was a time before the war. He could see Jackson and himself following a forest trail and finding a vixen and her kit foxes. A swamp of plump late-summer cattails. And, once, a school of silver carp.

His father was in the dream memory too. His father and his mother. Long ago when they were all together and had a home.

Stephen awoke with blades of sunlight blazing through the shutters. His father was gone. The racket of generators and pile drivers shattered the peace of the morning. He got out of bed and got dressed. When he looked outside, he could see that the night's dusting of snow had already begun to melt. The walkways and streets were filled with bustling soldiers and civilians, all looking as if they had somewhere important to go.

All he could think of was the accident. The accident that was part of the secret.

Sewa had a breakfast of roasted oats and wild

berries waiting for him on the massive oak slab that was the dining-room table. The morning newspapers, the *Santa Fe Times* and the *Santa Fe Sun*, lay messed on a chair.

"Your father left for work," she said. "He wants you to take a few days to adjust to the base before starting school. The only thing you must do today is stop at the hospital for your shots."

"What shots?"

"They have to make certain you won't get any bugs on base."

"I've had enough shots."

"Yes, I'm sure. But they're going to want to check you anyway. There's no time for anyone to be sick at Los Alamos."

"There doesn't seem to be much time for anything around here."

"That's not true. There's a gym and sports program in the rec hall. There are movies four times a week and ice-skating in North Canyon. Lots of stuff."

For a while after breakfast, Stephen sat in his room working on his journal and stringing up a B-29 to hang with his other planes. He pasted in a couple of the morning's newspaper articles on the war, ones about President Roosevelt and Prime Minister Churchill. He made an entry of his own for the day: *Los Alamos: February 24, 1945—Accident last night. Worried for Dad.*

When it was time to head out, Sewa stopped him at the door. "Stephen, remember to be careful," she said, checking to make certain his I.D. was pinned on right.

"Hey, Sewa, this isn't the first secret project I've been around, you know."

Stephen put on his coat and wrapped a scarf around his neck. Outside, there was a different M.P., a tall, blond crew-cut man, in front of Robert Oppenheimer's house. Another M.P. was patrolling across the street.

"Hi," Stephen said to the blond man.

The guard gave him a wave.

Stephen headed along a frosted boardwalk toward the perimeter fence. From there he could see the panorama of the distant mountains. A blanket of sagebrush and stunted junipers had grown back on the graded hillsides.

Beyond the scrub were tall piñon trees and a thick forest.

There was heavy traffic on the approach roads, troop trucks and earthmovers gasping their way up the steep grade. "Good morning," he said to a crane operator on a break.

"Hi," the man said.

Stephen let the man take a few sips of his coffee and then asked about what he really wanted to know:

"I heard there was an accident last night. Did you hear anything about it?" The smile faded from the driver's face.

"I didn't know there was one," the man said finally. The driver turned his back on Stephen, took his coffee, and climbed back up on his rig.

Stephen shifted his weight from one foot to the other a couple of times, then decided to clear out. He took a central boardwalk until he reached the double fence of the Tech Area. The dog transport truck was parked inside the gate. A strange boy in jeans, with straight black hair to his shoulder blades, was helping the redheaded burly man and old woman load a shift of dogs into the truck. The boy nodded hello.

"Hey there," the kid said, breaking into a wide smile. "You're new around here, right?"

"Yeah."

"I saw you coming in the gate yesterday. I figured I'd see you in school."

Stephen could see the boy was a couple of years older than he was, with green eyes like a wolf.

"I'm on my way to get my shots," Stephen said.

"Oh, yeah. Watch out for Nurse Klass, the Blind Barbarian. She'll stick you three, four times before she finds a vein."

"Great."

The boy leaned on the fence. "You know, if you say you need me to show you around, my dad'll let me off. I've had enough dogs and school for the day."

"Sure."

"Hey, Dad," the boy called out. "He's new. I'm gonna show him the hospital." The man gave a wave. The boy went to an access gate, punched a number code into the lock, and came out. "The hospital's near the north commissary, the one that has a soda fountain," he told Stephen. "I work there sometimes when one of the Pueblo orderlies doesn't show up. They empty the bedpans. I don't do bedpans." He led the way onto a plank walkway. "My name's Alexei."

"I'm Stephen."

"Where'd you come from?"

"London."

"You sound American."

"My Mom's English," Stephen said. "It's my dad who's from the States. Have the dogs ever caught any spies?"

"Nope. Just lost campers from Frijoles Canyon." Alexei took a running start, then jumped over a strip of slush to the next walkway. He was older, but Stephen's legs were longer. He jumped after him.

"My dad's housekeeper keeps warning me about kidnappers."

"The physicists are the only ones anyone's worried about. And their kids, like you."

"I didn't say I was the son of a physicist."

"You *look* it. Which one's your dad?"

Stephen hesitated. "Olaf," he said, finally.

Alexei laughed out loud.

Stephen laughed too.

Alexei picked up the pace. "We've got our dogs in kennels out along the Rio Grande. They wanted the barking off base. We've got good riding horses, too."

"Did you hear about the accident last night?" Stephen asked.

"Yes."

"I saw the guy. They checked him with Geiger counters." Stephen jumped across to another walkway. It felt good to have someone to talk to again.

Alexei tossed his head, making his hair fan out behind him. "Don't you want to know what's going on? What they're making? I know one guy who thinks it's a flying wing that can stay up for years without having to land. A lot of others think it's a new type of sub."

They reached a long, narrow building that looked like a bowling alley.

"This is it," Alexei said.

Inside the hospital was a glass partition in front of a brown metal desk. A nurse was standing in the corridor talking with a lieutenant.

"Hey, Miss Klass," Alexei called out to her. "You've got a new victim."

6

The nurse peered at them over her tortoiseshell glasses. Her bleached-blond hair swelled out from the sides of her cap like large earmuffs. "Hold your horses, Alexei."

"Is the Barbarian the only nurse?" Stephen asked, sitting down on a bench.

"She's the only one on morning shift."

Four men in suits, one with a stethoscope around his neck, came down the hall. A couple of them gave a wave to the nurse as they went out the front door.

"They fly specialists in from a Texas Air Force

base and Houston Methodist Hospital. Last month Groves brought in a surgeon to work on a guy who got three of his fingers blown off in the west canyon. They set off explosions over there. Not big ones, but enough to whack out an eye."

When the lieutenant left, Nurse Klass slipped behind the nurses' station, sat in a desk chair, and dialed a phone.

Alexei called out, "Hey, we don't have all day!"

The nurse swiveled so her back was to him.

"She'll be on for hours," Alexei said. "Come on—I'll show you around." He started down a corridor on the right.

Stephen got up and followed. Halfway down the hallway was an area with wheelchairs and stainless-steel tables. What looked like a big pressure cooker sat in a corner. Steam rolled out of it, creeping along the white tile of the floor.

"That's an autoclave," Alexei said. "It sterilizes scalpels and tongs. Syringes and test tubes, too."

Stephen glanced through the open doors as they passed a row of rooms. The rooms were empty, except for beds covered by sheets.

Alexei stopped at a doorway. A gray bed with metal side rails jutted out from the wall. Faded shades were half drawn over casement windows. Stephen recognized the patient cranked up in the bed, a man with a dazed and flushed face, staring at them.

Alexei gave the man a wave. "Okay if we come in?"

"We'd better not," Stephen told Alexei. "That's the guy who was wrapped in the aluminum."

Alexei went in anyway. Stephen stayed at the doorway. Bags of liquid hung from a silvery rack next to the bed, colorless drippings inching down through a tube. A syringe needle was taped in place on the back of the man's left hand.

"Are you okay?" Alexei asked.

The man looked at him, then at Stephen.

"I was waiting," the man said. His voice was small. Shaky. "Waiting for . . . you."

Alexei checked the intravenous drips. "They've got him on morphine. He's probably on the moon. His name's Soifer. I've seen him chowing down at the commissary. Dr. Soifer. He's a physicist."

Soifer looked toward the windows. "Is my suit there? Where are my shoes?"

"We ought to get out of here," Stephen said.

Alexei acted like he hadn't heard. He put his hand on the bed railing. "What happened in the lab? What was the accident?"

Stephen was shocked Alexei was quizzing the dazed man. "We shouldn't be in his room. You can't ask him—"

"We were doing an experiment," Soifer said. His face was gaunt. "We were tired from the long hours. We had been working too hard. There was the fuel—"

"What fuel?" Alexei wanted to know.

Soifer took a deep breath. He shuddered. "Too much for a drop. We were letting it fall, letting it go critical for a split second—"

"I'm leaving," Stephen said. He started for the door. Soifer began to slap his own hip, smack it as though he were trying to swat at something crawling under his skin. Alexei reached out to the control for the morphine drip.

Stephen halted. "What are you *doing*?"

"Giving him more."

"More morphine?"

"Yes."

"You can't do that."

Soifer gasped. After a moment the increase of the morphine drip seemed to make the pain fade. He spoke again. "The Tail of the Tiger . . ."

"What is that, Dr. Soifer?" Alexei pressed. "What's the Tail of the Tiger?"

"What we called it . . . the experiment. We knew something could go wrong . . . that it was like a wild animal . . ."

Soifer was staring at Stephen now. The man's mouth opened, like he was trying to tell Stephen a secret.

Stephen was drawn closer. He knew he shouldn't. He knew it was something that wasn't right, but there were things he wanted to know. Had to know.

"Find out what happened," Alexei said. "Pump him."

"I'm Olaf's son," Stephen whispered to Soifer. "Olaf is my father. . . ."

Soifer began to choke. He pointed toward a sink in the corner of the room. "Water . . . my face is burning. I'm burning . . ."

"Get the nurse," Stephen told Alexei.

Alexei hesitated.

"*Now,*" Stephen said.

Alexei turned and headed out of the room and down the corridor. Soifer struggled to grasp a metal pitcher on his bed stand.

"I understand," Stephen said. He took the pitcher and filled it from the sink tap. Soifer pushed a shallow steel tray toward him. Stephen half filled it with water. The man tried to dip a washcloth, nearly spilling the whole tray.

Stephen took the cloth from his hands, wrung it out, and pressed it gently on Soifer's brow. He didn't want to ask anything more, but a question crawled inside him. It had been there from the moment he had arrived at Los Alamos. It was there now. More than anything.

"What is the secret here? The race, Dr. Soifer . . . the big secret?"

Soifer glared at him. He coughed and looked as though he were thinking things through himself—as if he were fighting his way up through fear. Then, suddenly, he thrust his body to the right until he was hanging over the aluminum rail. Stephen caught him, but not before he had knocked a thermometer and a tray of bandages from the top of his bed stand and plunged his hand into the drawer.

"Sir, you've got to sit up," Stephen said. "Stay in the bed or you're going to hurt yourself. If you want something, I'll get it for you."

Stephen got Soifer to lean back against the pillows. "They'll tie you into the bed," he said as he checked to make certain the intravenous tubes and connections were all still in place. He could see Soifer still wanted something.

"Something from in *here*?" Stephen asked, indicating the drawer.

"Yes."

Stephen opened the drawer. There was only a pair of strange, thick sunglasses. "These what you want?" Stephen said.

Soifer nodded.

Stephen picked up the sunglasses and tried to hand them to Soifer. Soifer pushed them back at him.

"Gadget," he said.

Stephen leaned closer. "What did you say?"

"We call it the *Gadget*."

The man's face twisted into a grimace. "You keep the glasses."

"No, I can't."

Stephen tried to put the glasses back into the bed stand. Soifer cried out, "You keep them. *You* need them."

Stephen glanced toward the doorway hoping to see that Alexei and the nurse had come, but they hadn't. There was silence in the hallway. Stephen turned back to Soifer and put on the strange glasses. Their blue-black tint was so dark, he could hardly see through the lenses.

"Keep them," Soifer demanded.

"I can't."

"Please."

Stephen thought a moment. "I'll tell you what I'll do," he said, finally. "I'll hold them for you—save them until you get well." He took off the glasses, carefully folded them, and put them into his coat pocket. "I'll hold them until you get out of here. Okay?"

Soifer tugged at the rumpled sheets and

began to slap his thigh again. "Help me," he said.

"What?"

"I've dirtied myself. . . ."

Stephen saw the stains creeping through the folds of the sheets.

"Please . . . clean me. . . ."

Alexei was in the doorway.

"Where's the nurse?" Stephen asked.

"Still talking the legs off a chair."

"You stay with him," Stephen said to Alexei. He put the washcloth down and walked out. There were sounds in the hallway: a baby crying somewhere; other patients in distant rooms, some coughing like they had the flu; people talking. Nurse Klass swiveled in her chair at the nurses' station. She was still on the phone.

Laughing.

"Excuse me," Stephen said.

Klass glanced at him, waved him off, and turned her full attention back to the phone. Stephen said, "The patient, Dr. Soifer, he's had an accident. I'm sorry. He needs to be cleaned. . . ."

She motioned for him to go away. She was

talking to someone about seeing *Going My Way*, and there were plans for a picnic on Saturday. There would be hiking in Diablo Canyon, and she would bring wine from the PX.

At first Stephen wasn't aware that he was shouting. The anger had come suddenly roaring up out of him. "WASH HIM. YOU HANG UP AND YOU WASH HIM. YOU CLEAN HIM NOW. YOU HEAR ME! YOU CLEAN HIM.

"NOW.

"NOW."

The nurse went silent and stared at him. Her hands were shaking as she laid the phone down onto its cradle. Keeping an eye on Stephen, she stood. A moment longer and Stephen had control of himself again. The adrenaline was still pumping. His heart hurt in his chest. He'd never yelled before like that at anyone.

Never.

Klass headed down the hallway toward Soifer's room.

"Thank you," Stephen said as he followed after her. "Thank you very much.

"There's your shots," Nurse Klass told Stephen. "If you have any reaction, let me know."

Klass hadn't reported him or Alexei, and they, in turn, hadn't reported her. Alexei had threatened to tell everything lazy and slipshod and incompetent about her if she did try to make any trouble.

Stephen had watched the nurse's face as she appeared to be considering the best course of action. He could almost hear her thinking: *Right. Well, we'll just all hush up about it. We've thought it over and—we don't want anything going on anyone's record. No yellow slips into anyone's file . . .*

"They're building something called the Gadget," Stephen told Alexei as they walked back down the main street.

"Is that what Soifer said?"

"Yes." He took the glasses out of his pocket and flashed them to Alexei. "He gave me these."

"Sunglasses?"

"Ones you can hardly see through."

"Guys on morphine will do and say anything. I was at the hospital one night, and a patient kept telling me he was going to give me his car, and that God was sitting on the end of his bed."

"I don't think Soifer was kidding about the Gadget."

"Now I really have to find out what's going on around here." Alexei looked like he'd slipped and shown more interest than he wanted to. He gave Stephen a playful punch in his arm.

Stephen managed a laugh.

"Somebody's got to know what they're making," Stephen said. "Someone who's not drugged and lying helpless in a hospital."

"We gotta take what we can get," Alexei said.

"Everybody else clams up."

"Most of the kids around here don't care. They don't even think it's weird that everyone has to get their mail from a P.O. box that's in another *town*. My dad thinks half of Santa Fe's a front for this place—especially 109 East Palace Avenue. There's supposed to be some old lady there who has the scientists in for tea, and they drive away with Montgomery Ward washing machines and all kinds of gifts from the Army."

Stephen slipped the sunglasses back into his jacket pocket, nodding.

"But you and me together," Alexei said, narrowing his wolf eyes. "I'll bet we'll find out everything."

But how come you make it sound like a vow? Stephen thought.

Stephen tried to forget about Dr. Soifer for the next few days. Forget the nurse and the yelling and everything that was scary about it. Friday was his first day at the base school. There were eight classrooms, four for the lower grades and four for the high school. All the lower grades had to double up.

Alexei stopped by Bathtub Row to walk to school with Stephen. "Feel like going riding today?" Alexei said. "You've been on horses, right?"

"Yeah."

"Good."

On the way to school Alexei waved to an older boy wearing a beret and zoot-suit jacket. Stephen recognized the boy, Jason Matuzawitz, from Chicago. He had always thought Jason looked crazy, with a hairline that cut across the front of his brow like he'd had brain surgery—and he was always doing things like throwing rocks at kids or stealing from drugstores.

"Jason says he knows you," Alexei said to Stephen.

"Yeah," Stephen said as the bell rang.

"See you after class," Alexei said. Alexei went across the hall to catch up with Jason, and the two of them went into the sophomore classroom.

Stephen hoped Alexei wasn't as good a friend of Jason's as it looked like. He went into his classroom, and the teacher, Mrs. Haines, closed the door. Mrs. Haines was short and wore a dress with polka dots. Stephen gave her the sealed envelope with his London school records in it. His father had told him Mrs. Haines was a great teacher and married to the base butcher.

"Let's welcome Stephen," Mrs. Haines announced to the class.

Several of the kids mumbled hello as he took his seat. One wall of the room had a large window with a beautiful view of Jemez Canyon and the Nacimiento Mountains. Stephen recognized two more kids from the Army school in Chicago. One kid, Ricky Puliese, had always breathed with his mouth open like a gasping fish. He had always asked questions, and he never knew when to shut up.

"Nicole has brought in her pet today," Mrs. Haines said.

A skinny girl stood up holding a Moroccan chest that was inlaid with small curls of silver wire. "The chest is for snakes," Nicole said as she took a boa constrictor out of it. "The man I bought it from in Marrakech kept cobras in it."

The boy behind Steven leaned forward and whispered in his ear. "We call her 'Mouse.' That's what she feeds her snake. She sleeps with mice, too."

"Thanks for letting me know," Stephen said.

After school Alexei was waiting for Stephen at the end of the hallway. "I know a shortcut to the stables," Alexei said.

"I'm not supposed to go off base."

"It's okay. We can ride out to my dad's ranch. Dad'll drive you home after our ride. It's safe. The Army runs the stables."

Alexei led the way along the perimeter fence of the canyon. "This'll save us a half-mile hike and getting passes," he said, lifting a bottom strip of the chain link.

"What about the M.P.s?"

"They don't come back here. They've got privates to feed the horses and shovel out the stalls. They make them do anything they want."

Stephen lay down on the ground and rolled under the fence. Then he held it up for Alexei.

"Oppie's wife keeps her horse at the stables, too," Alexei said. "I see her riding in the canyons with one of the other wives, who's married to the head of the Ordnance Division."

"How come you know what everyone does?" Stephen asked.

Alexei laughed. "Give yourself a few weeks and you'll be a know-it-all too."

Stephen followed Alexei to a brook. The flowing water was warm, steaming. The ground all around was frozen except where the brook flowed.

"It's spillage from the Tech Area," Alexei said. "Whatever that Gadget is, it makes the water hot. Who knows what's in it!"

Strands of elodea moved like eels in the current. Clumps of fern and skunk cabbage covered the banks. Stephen squatted to get a closer look at the frogs and tadpoles scooting through the water. He shot his hand out to grab one.

"Don't," Alexei said.

It was too late. Stephen had cupped one of

the frogs in his palms. He yelled and dropped it. "Hey, it's got two heads!"

"Yeah," Alexei said. "There's a lot of two-headed reptiles and fish all along here. That's one thing they're making, okay. Two-headed snakes. There are freaks all around Los Alamos. One day there's a hillside of giant flowers. The next day all the flowers are dead."

They hiked for a ways along a wide arroyo and then up a steep slope to the stables.

"Hey, Logan," Alexei called out to one of the stable workers. The private waved back as Alexei took Stephen into one of the stalls. A large black gelding and a red-dappled filly looked up. "This is Crazy and Smally. You're going to ride Smally. She's calmer than Crazy."

"I figured," Stephen said. He reached out to pet Smally. She turned her head and licked his hand.

They saddled up the horses and mounted them. Alexei led the way out of the main paddock. Stephen held Smally's reins loosely. He leaned forward onto the saddle horn and smoothed her mane.

By the time they reached the canyon rim, Smally was snorting and lifting her legs high, as though she were glad to have Stephen on board. When Stephen saw how deep the gorge was, he was grateful there was a high chain-link fence between the riding trail and the drop. "They've got the fence up for a reason, I suppose."

"Yeah," Alexei said. "A couple of people have gone over. Farther along there's no fence, and sometimes one of the locals will have a problem. If you see a bouquet of dried flowers and a cross on the rim, you know that's where there was an accident. That someone died there."

On the main trail Stephen signaled Smally into a lope. When he passed Alexei, Crazy changed stride, too. The gorge curved, its time lines of eroded sandstone defined sharply, like tide stains on a bulkhead. The late-afternoon sun made Smally's coat gleam red like fire. Still farther on, a troop of magpies took to the air. Chipmunks crossed the riding trail in a dither.

Stephen felt confident on the horse. It was

the first time he'd gone riding since last summer, which he'd spent with Jackson. The fence ahead bordered a straightaway. Stephen urged Smally faster. The canyon wind whipped at Stephen's hair and jacket. He noticed Smally's ears going back, flattening the way horses' do when they're angry.

"What's the matter, girl?" Stephen said. "It's okay—"

Smally broke into a gallop.

"Hey, be careful," Alexei yelled from behind, as he gave Crazy free rein to keep up.

Stephen enjoyed the speed for a stretch, but the ride grew rough, and Stephen pulled on the reins. Smally turned her head from side to side, checking who was riding her. Her racing hoofs pounded the clay and pebbles of the trail.

"Pull her in," Alexei shouted.

Now the horse was traveling dangerously fast. Stephen held on to the horn and pulled back harder, but Smally still poured on the speed.

"I'm trying to stop her!" Stephen yelled. The horse galloped closer to the wire fence.

"Turn her," Alexei called.

Stephen fought to get the horse away from the fence and the edge of the canyon, but she went nearer still. "She's trying to rub me off," he cried. He pulled on the reins with all his strength. He tried yanking Smally's head away from the fence and the drop to the river on the right.

Stephen heard Crazy gaining on them as Alexei dug his heels into the gelding's flanks.

"What should I do?" Stephen called out.

"Pull her head toward the fence," Alexei shouted. "Toward it."

Smally was listing. Stephen's leg was within an inch of the wire mesh. If his leg hit the fence, he knew it would be like having it pressed into a grater.

"Toward it!" came Alexei's voice again. *"Yank her!"*

Stephen tugged the reins hard to the right. He pulled until his arms hurt and the horse's head was closer to the fence than his leg was. It would be Smally's head being broken or ripped open, not his leg. Another moment, and Smally seemed to get the point and veered away. She slowed into a frisky trot.

"Nice work," Alexei said, catching up to Stephen's side. "You showed her who's boss."

"Nothing to it," Stephen said, as he leaned forward and patted Smally to let her know he was onto her game, but that she'd been forgiven.

Alexei led the way on Crazy for another mile along the gorge. The fence ended, and they followed the canyon rim past a grove of cottonwoods. Here the trail became narrow and gutted, with nothing between them and the edge of the abyss. A steel railroad bridge stretched out across the drop. Far below, the river ran white and narrow.

The blood drained from Stephen's face.

"The Rio Grande gorge is six hundred feet deep here," Alexei said. "There." He pointed off to the left. "That's my dad's ranch."

There was a cluster of buildings—a main house and five or six outbuildings and kennels. The barking of dogs started up from the fenced runs. A tall chain-link fence framed the rolling fields of scrub on three sides. The fourth barrier was the chasm itself.

They rode up to the ranch house and got off their mounts. Alexei tethered the horses at a water trough and ran for the kennels.

"Come on," Alexei called back to Stephen.

Stephen caught up as the barking became deafening. Thirty or forty German shepherds leaped against the fencing, their teeth flashing and tails wagging.

"Stephen is my friend," Alexei yelled to them. "My pal." He draped his arm over Stephen's shoulder so the dogs could see. "They won't hurt you now," Alexei said as he threw a switch that opened the kennel gates.

A dozen of the dogs rushed Stephen, jumping up on him and licking his face.

"Let's go!" Alexei yelled to the dogs. He started racing up the scrub hillside. Stephen and the dogs took off after him. The German shepherds circled the two boys. Leaping.

Howling.

"This is one place you can feel safe, good buddy," Alexei shouted over the din.

"Yes," Stephen said.

For the first time in a long while, Stephen threw out his hands and let himself spin in mindless circles.

March 1945
Four Months to Deadline

Stephen spent the next several afternoons after school at Alexei's ranch. Stephen and Alexei would ride the horses until sundown and then go inside. Alexei's whole family was friendly, and Mr. Nagavatsky, Alexei's father, was a good cook. Mr. Nagavatsky usually made barbecued beef ribs or chicken. One night the whole family just sat around the dinner table making baloney sandwiches and eating popcorn.

"I don't think Stephen should be riding in the canyons," Stephen overheard Sewa telling his father one night.

"I think it's okay. Mr. Nagavatsky drives him home."

"I still don't think it's safe."

"I'll talk with Mr. Nagavatsky and the boys," Stephen's father said. "Alexei could start coming over here."

Sewa made a face.

"What's the matter?"

"I'm not sure that's such a good idea either," Sewa said.

Stephen heard his father laugh. "Sewa, you sure are a tough cookie," he said.

It was over a month before Stephen received his first letter from his mother, and even then it was only because Oppenheimer had put his foot down with Groves. He demanded that from now on all the physicists' mail be uncensored and transported by special air pouch.

March 27

Dear Stephen,

Thank you for your letter. I'm fine, so don't worry about me. Everyone here misses you very much.

Stephen, things are difficult but hopeful here. The basement of our building has been made into a bomb shelter and school. Little Molly has started in a special class there and carries her books in a rucksack made out of a poultry feed bag. Your grandfather and grandmother have been stretching the family rations by queuing up to buy lots of apples and horsemeat, because no food coupons are needed for them. The meat tastes just fine in stew and meatloaf, and it's a great deal more tender than mutton.

I was upset to hear about Dad losing weight and not looking well. This happens to him when he has a long assignment and I'm not there. I'm thankful that he has you and Sewa to help take care of him. Make sure she packs a Hershey bar and a pear or cake in his bag when he goes to work in the morning. He wouldn't think to do it himself. I know his friend in Communications is working on a time for us to speak by radio or phone.

I have a little news about our family's plans here. I've decided to accept that everyone wants to stay in London to do their part in the war effort. Your aunt Shannon lasted three months in the country before she came back to work on the assembly line making Spitfires. It is so hard to believe that our few British planes and pilots could have so damaged the German air force. We understand it has driven Hitler quite mad. I mean that, literally.

Your aunt Jo is back too. She's part of a team that puts up the huge barrage balloons to help keep out whatever is left of the Luftwaffe. Cousin Clair mans an antiaircraft gun in Brighton. Your aunt Bess, arthritis and all, runs one of the trains and, on her day off, drives an ambulance. We're all doing whatever we can. Even the queen is pitching in, helping people in the streets and hospitals.

I know you will take care of Dad and help him get through this assignment. You must know he would like nothing more than to spend all his time with you. You remember how much he loved taking you bowling and having a catch with you. But his work is very important. You know what I mean.

Please be patient. I know Dad can be difficult, but he's under a pressure you and I can't really understand. Give him hugs for me, dear Stephen.

Love,
Mom

P.S. Okay. I hate the taste of horsemeat. No matter how it's seasoned, it still tastes like it should be pulling a coal cart.

The next week, Stephen convinced his father to let him stay the whole weekend at the Nagavatskys' ranch. Alexei's aunt Ludmila and one of the ranch hands made the dinner on Friday: breaded veal, dumplings, and lima beans. Alexei had told Stephen that Aunt Ludmila always wore long dresses because she had varicose veins and was ashamed of them. Saturday night Mr. Nagavatsky drove everyone down to a river beach in the gorge and roasted chicken and ribs, with potatoes buried in the hot coals until their skins were black and crispy.

Everyone ate and talked around the campfire. Mr. Nagavatsky's voice was low, with a soothing accent. Sometimes Aunt Ludmila and he would say something to each other in their native language, Russian. Alexei told a joke about a parrot that could sing "Dig You Later (A Hubba-Hubba-Hubba)." Aunt Ludmila recited a poem she'd written about men laying the first train tracks across the Sierra Nevada. Eventually everyone was talking about Los Alamos and the war and what kind of top-secret things could be going on in Santa Fe with the old lady at 109 East Palace Avenue.

"The newspapers and radio reports out of Germany say that Adolf Hitler's losing his mind," Mr. Nagavatsky said when things quieted down. He ran his fingers through his shock of red curly hair. "The closer our Allied forces get to Berlin, the nuttier things he's doing. His own officers try to escape."

"I guess the war's going to be over," Stephen said, not really thinking.

Aunt Ludmila brought out a tray of sliced fruit from a chiller and passed it around. "It would be nice if the war ended," she said. "Does your father think it's going to be soon too?"

Stephen realized maybe he shouldn't have said anything. "No," he said. "My dad doesn't tell me anything about anything. I hardly ever see him."

"The physicists are very busy over there," Mr. Nagavatsky said. "Everyone is."

After dinner Stephen stayed sitting around the fire with Mr. Nagavatsky while Alexei and the others took a walk along the bank of the river. The Rio Grande was less than fifty feet wide at this point in the gorge.

"What city in Russia did you come from?" Stephen asked Mr. Nagavatsky.

"My family bred wolfhounds in Guriev. They were almost two hundred pounds. Huge. Smart. That's where I learned to love dogs and train them. I've worked for the U.S. Army for many years."

"I like your accent."

"Thank you," Mr. Nagavatsky said. He smiled. "I'm glad Russia and the United States are friends and fighting on the same side. If I had some other kind of accent, I might end up in a detention camp, like they've done with the Japanese Americans. This is not a good time to be in America and have an accent."

Stephen moved closer to the fire.

"Mr. Nagavatsky," Stephen said. He lowered his voice so it wouldn't be carried by the wind. "Do you know what my father's working on? What everyone is doing at Los Alamos?"

Stephen could see Mr. Nagavatsky was studying him carefully.

"I don't know," Mr. Nagavatsky said. "I only hope it will not be the last of the Dark Angels to visit upon the earth." He smiled. "My old church in Russia believes that when the seventh angel comes, it will be the death of our planet."

"What kind of Dark Angels?" Stephen asked.

"Six have come already," Mr. Nagavatsky said. He moved next to Stephen. "The first were ice and flood. Then glaciers melting. Next came pestilence—rats and locusts—vermin—and drought. Sometimes I get the order of the angels a little mixed up. But the fifth Dark Angel is believed to be the pollution of our waters, which has already begun. The sixth Dark Angel is war and the masks we give it. All the wars since the beginning of time. Slaughterings and the cruelty of man to man."

"What's the seventh Dark Angel?" Stephen asked.

"Ah, no one will know for certain until that angel has arrived," Mr. Nagavatsky said. "The church says this seventh angel will come soon. It is the angel from which the earth will not be able to recover. Death's feast and the end of life. Let's hope the summoning of this Dark Angel is not the ambition of Los Alamos."

Stephen couldn't forget the terror he'd seen in Dr. Soifer's eyes. Sometimes Soifer would come to him in a dream. He would be in a wheelchair, reaching out, trying to hit him with his fist or a stick. Stephen wished he could talk to Dr. Soifer again.

Questions.

There were more questions to be asked.

The next Sunday, Stephen's father said they should go on the weekly hike with the other families. Stephen started out walking with his father's arm around his shoulder. It felt good to be out together. The whole inner circle of physicists and their families had turned out, as usual, for the outing on their day off. The day was as warm as summer as they started into Bandelier Canyon. Everyone was laughing and lugging backpacks loaded with sandwiches and sodas.

For a while Stephen felt happy.

"One Sunday we saw a cougar," his father said. "There's always a group of wolves or a coyote. A few mountain sheep up on the ridges."

About a half mile up the canyon, Oppenheimer—wearing his porkpie hat—and Bainbridge had begun to walk ahead of the others. Stephen felt his father's hand slip away from him. Soon his father and most of the other scientists were walking a couple of hundred feet in front of their families.

Kids began to peel off and throw rocks down the side of the canyon trail. Most of the wives were soon left in their own group trailing far behind. Stephen didn't like what had happened. He wasn't about to join Jason Matuzawitz's group. The older boys finally dropped back behind the wives to sneak a smoke.

Two of the girls next to him were singing "On the Atchison, Topeka, and the Santa Fe" and kicking in a chorus line. He'd known Sabrina from Chicago. Her father was on the same technical team as his dad. She always had a friendly smile.

"Hey, Brini," Stephen said.

"Hi, Stephen. Did you hear about Nicole?" she asked.

"The one who sleeps with mice and then feeds them to her snake?"

"Yeah." Libby Birman laughed, joining the huddle. "She was going to come on the hike, but she's so weird."

"What happened?"

"She rolled over in bed last night and accidentally killed two of her mice," Sabrina said.

The girls made Stephen laugh. Farther along on the trail, he took Sabrina off to one side. "I want to ask you something, Brini."

"What?"

"This place is so weird. I can't help wondering—what's so important around here that our dads are hardly ever home? What do they do? What're they working on?"

"I don't ask."

Libby had caught up to them and overheard Stephen's question. "Who cares?" she said. "I don't think they know what they're doing. They all work on separate pieces. That way it's a nice big puzzle that nobody knows the answers to. I can't wait until it's over." She took a deep breath. "I just heard now that it was *three* mice Mouse Girl crushed."

Up ahead his father had turned back to look at him. He had one of his *Oh, you be nice and make friends now* looks on his face.

Stephen was glad when Alexei started the next week to come over to Bathtub Row after school. Sewa was there when they came in. Once she made an apricot pie. Stephen had begun to build a model destroyer from a kit he'd found at the PX. Alexei helped trim the pieces of balsa wood and passed the pieces to Stephen. Whenever they got tired of model building, they'd switch to work on Stephen's journal. Alexei clipped out the articles and photos Stephen had marked in new magazines, and Stephen pasted them in.

Stephen had divided his journal by years. He kept important headlines: "Mussolini Deposed"; "Italy Surrenders to America's General Eisenhower" . . .

Alexei read every word of the journal, even Stephen's personal handwritten entries. Lately Stephen had copied reports he'd gotten from the radio into the journal.

"It's clear that we're winning the war," Alexei said. He had begun to study Stephen's collection of war-machine trading cards. A German U-boat. Aircraft carriers. Japanese gunboats. "So why is everyone working so hard around here? Even if we end up making this Gadget thing, why do they want it?"

Stephen remembered the fright on Soifer's face when he had handed him the pair of special sunglasses. He could still hear his voice. *You keep the glasses.* You *need them* . . .

Like a warning.

Pushing the glasses on him.

"Whatever it is, maybe Hitler's making it too," Stephen said. "Half the scientists at Los Alamos are from Germany. They got out before Hitler held all the others and forced them to work for him. If the scientists here know how to make it, then the ones who stayed in Germany have got to be trying to make the same thing, too."

"You know," Alexei said, "if it is a new kind of sub, it'd be a little weird to build it in these mountains."

"You're right. You'd build a sub in Oregon or Maine. Some place that has an ocean."

"A man here from Oak Ridge told my dad that whatever they're making there in Tennessee, they're hiding it under forty-two acres of roof. That could cover a dozen aircraft carriers."

"Hitler's losing the war," Stephen said.

"Not if he gets the Gadget first."

There was a sound at the door. They looked up to see Sewa staring at them. "I think Alexei should go now," Sewa said.

Stephen didn't argue.

After Alexei left, Stephen confronted Sewa.

"What's going to make you happy?" Stephen asked. "When I don't have any friends at all?"

"I'm sorry," Sewa said sadly.

"But why doesn't Sewa like Alexei?" Stephen asked. "He's my friend."

"You know, he is older than you. I didn't tell her I agreed with her. I told her I thought Alexei was a fine boy." His father sat across from him at the dining-room table finishing the last of a baked-chicken-and-rice casserole that Sewa had left for them. She had gone home to her pueblo for the night.

"She also thinks he has secrets," his father said. "That there are things Alexei is not telling us. I don't think she believes he's a bad kid. She has good instincts, son. You and I don't have to always like everything. We don't have to know all the answers. Sewa is only interested in our safety."

"From what?"

"There recently was a kidnapping in Chicago. One of the scientists' daughters was taken."

"Who?"

"It doesn't matter who. His daughter was five years old. They did things to her. Things I can't tell you about."

"Then why are you telling me at all?"

"Stephen, if anyone ever tries to take you, you run and you run! You *never* let them get you alone. Do you understand?"

"Yes, Dad. I understand."

A week later Stephen waited until dinner was over before he told his father: "Mrs. Haines and Mr. Liebowitz, the shop teacher, are taking us on a class trip to the Santa Fe annual jamboree. Actually, it'll be half the school. All the lower grades and teachers, and a couple of the kids' mothers."

"I suppose it's all right," his father said, after thinking a moment. "If you promise to be very careful. The Fermis and I went last year. It's very crowded. What's the school doing for safety?"

"There's going to be a slew of chaperons, and we have to use a buddy system. Everybody's been assigned a partner. Mrs. Haines said they've got rodeo events, and you can ride a camel. A tent with geodes and petrified wood. And I want to see the trained doves that take money out of your hand and give you a rolled-up piece of paper with your fortune on it."

His father stared at him as though he suspected Stephen was leaving something out. Stephen knew if he said what was really on his mind, his father would never let him out of the house. *Oh yes, Dad, I'm really more interested in checking out a P.O. box where everyone on base is supposed to live. And I'll throw in 109 East Palace Avenue, too.*

"I'll be careful. Everybody's going."

The morning of the trip, Stephen went to school early and boarded the school bus with his class. His appointed buddy, Nicole, was a no-show.

"She probably rolled over in bed and killed another mouse," Stephen said.

"Those stories aren't even true," Mrs. Haines said. "She feeds the mice to her snake; she doesn't roll over on them."

"Yes, she does." He winked.

Mrs. Haines laughed. "Well, you team up with

some of the others. It's going to be very crowded."

The bus wove its way down the steep road and crossed the bridge spanning the Rio Grande. Stephen was sorry he had taken a window seat. He had forgotten they had to cross the gorge. The drop. His fear of height.

Jackson . . .

In Santa Fe, sunshine painted the rows of adobe houses, with their glazed, tiled roofs and patios. Brightly colored Indian and Spanish shops sat next to stores like Woolworth's and a U.S. Tire outlet. The bus passed down narrow winding streets lined with adobe façades. Santa Fe's river flowed violently from the thawing of snow on the lower slopes of the Sangre de Cristo Mountains.

"Our bus leaves to go back at four o'clock sharp," Mrs. Haines announced as the driver set the brake and opened the bus doors. "Pickup is in front of the Cristo Rey Church. If you get lost, just ask for the Cristo. Everybody knows it."

Stephen made certain he was the last one off the bus. It had been his plan from the beginning—to get off on his own and check out everything he wanted to. With Nicole out of the picture, it would all be easier. It took him only a few minutes to ditch the rest of the class.

There were so many people in the streets that he felt safe. If anybody tried to pull anything, it'd be easy enough to yell. Oil paintings of eggs and bowls of fruit seemed to be in every shop window. Bronze horse sculptures and grotesque masks stared out at him from private, fenced gardens. Indians in animal headdresses—twirling cloaks trimmed with ermine tails and eagle feathers—rode horses past the Palace of the Governors. In the corners of the main plaza, groups of Pueblo and other Indian tribes were performing creation-myth dances and chanting. A man next to Stephen was calling out:

Coyote shaped the first people of our world from the mud. And Raven told them to rise from a clam shell because he was lonely. . . .

Indian women chanted and clapped. They wore moccasins with beadwork and mirror inserts.

Stephen nearly walked past the post office, his main objective. It looked more like a private home, but inside were the usual counters and desks with pens. He found Box 1663 in a wall of mailboxes. It had a glass window like all the other boxes and a dial combination lock.

He was peering through the little window of the P.O. box when he noticed two monks watching him. Their hoods were up. Metal crucifixes hung from their waists.

Monks.

Stephen walked quickly to the wide-open stamp window.

"Can you tell me where East Palace Avenue is?" Stephen asked one of the Indian clerks.

"Sure." The man pointed to a street map under the glass countertop. "You're *here*," he said, "and you want to go *there*."

"Thanks," Stephen said.

Outside, Stephen walked against the flow of the crowd. A high school band had started down the street playing "Too-Ra-Loo-Ra-Loo-Ra." Mariachis were playing "Tico Tico" with trumpets and a fifteen-foot xylophone on wheels.

As Stephen moved along a stretch of adobe wall, there were stalls with Indians selling turquoise and parkas made from deerskin. Men and women were shouting to pull tourists into games of chance with dice made from animal teeth. He decided to pick up his pace. There was too much hawking. And suddenly a feeling that something wasn't right.

He looked around, but there was nothing. The next street had to be East Palace Avenue, and he was trying to remember the map. Trying to remember if he had to turn left.

Or was 109 to the right?

He noticed an old maroon Packard station wagon pulling up next to him at the curb. He couldn't help noticing that a monk was driving, and another man with a hood sat in the backseat. He looked behind him. The two monks from the post office were walking fast toward him. He was between the adobe wall and the Packard when suddenly one of the monks on the sidewalk was holding him tightly by his arm. The monk's other hand held a knife, with an intricately carved handle of bone or ivory.

"Get in the car," the monk ordered. He had an accent. Not German or anything Stephen could be certain of. He shoved Stephen toward the rear door of the station wagon.

Another pair of arms reached out and grabbed him.

"HELP," Stephen shouted. "HELP ME."

The marching band was deafening. He heard his father's stern voice in his head: *You never let them get you alone.*

Stephen spun violently, and he kicked at the man with the knife. As he bolted backward, he heard the ripping of a robe and the bang of metal as his foot struck the side of the wagon.

Run.

You run and you run!

He heard the shout of men's voices behind him. The monks were coming after him. He screamed for help again, but his voice was drowned in the boom of drums. There were tourists and Indians and kids in cowboy hats. People stared at him and the hooded monks who were after him.

They saw what was going on.

They laughed. A flight of clowns. Some kind of a joke. It was all part of the parade.

The crowd was too thick. The hooded men were going to catch him.

"This way," a familiar voice cried out.

Stephen hadn't seen the boy running alongside the wall. The boy in blue jeans and Army boots and long raven hair. He followed the boy into an alley that opened on the right. It was another moment before he knew for certain that he was following Alexei.

Two of the monks raced into the alley after them. Alexei dashed across a courtyard and up a rickety porch staircase two steps at a time. Stephen ran after him.

Somehow Stephen managed to reach the top floor before the stomping of the men's feet started rocking the staircase.

Alexei was ahead of Stephen, tearing along a stretch of balcony on the second floor. Stephen strained to keep up. Two of the monks were still chasing after them. Alexei held open a door, and now they were climbing higher. One flight of stairs, and then a turn. Another flight, and suddenly the shadowy hallway burst into light. They were out a door onto a rooftop.

"Hurry!" Alexei shouted.

Stephen ran ahead to the end of the roof—and stopped. The parade and crowd were four stories below. Another mariachi band made its trumpets scream. When Stephen looked up, he saw Alexei balancing on several planks that reached from one rooftop across to another.

"Come on," Alexei called.

"I can't."

"Yes, you can."

"No."

Stephen began to call down toward the crowd for help. Huge white faces with monstrous black eyes seemed to be staring up at him, but they were only the blind head masks of kachina spirits. Dancers, wearing skulls that streamed with strands of grass, stamped and shouted.

A ceremonial war dance had begun.

BANG.

Fireworks began to explode at the riverbank.

Now the two men in hoods were on the roof, running toward him.

Stephen turned and saw Alexei hurrying back for him. Alexei grabbed him and was making him move out onto the planks—walking, balancing on the narrow boards.

"I'm going to fall," Stephen said.

"Hold on to me," Alexei said.

In the street below, children set off Roman candles, trails of blazing magnesium and white smoke. *Stephen was back on the rooftop in London. He was with Jackson at the edge of a building. . . .*

For just a moment . . .

Then:

Alexei had Stephen across onto the other roof. He pulled him behind a wall. Quickly, Alexei ran back and slid the planks away from the edge, sending them crashing down into an alleyway.

The bridge and the robed men were gone. It was as if the men had disappeared.

Suddenly.

Too fast.

Alexei was back at his side before Stephen could begin to get his breath back and start to believe that he *might* be safe again.

"Where did you come from?" Stephen asked Alexei. "How'd you find me?"

"Later," Alexei said. "We've got to get off this building pronto in case those guys didn't give up."

When Stephen and Alexei came down from the roof on a rusted iron fire escape, they found themselves at the edge of the plaza.

"I wasn't going to miss out on a day at a jamboree with you, good buddy," Alexei said. "I told them at school that one of the patrol dogs had gone crazier than a loon, and my dad wanted me to take care of it. It wasn't hard to figure out you'd be someplace around the P.O. or on East Palace Avenue."

Alexei led Stephen to a pair of M.P.s in front of La Fonda, a fancy hotel.

"Someone tried to kidnap me," Stephen said. "Monks in robes . . . they had a Packard . . . a maroon station wagon . . ."

"Whoa," the shorter of the two M.P.s said.

"I'm Dr. Orr's son . . . Mr. Olaf . . ."

"We're from Site Y," Alexei said quickly. "Guys were really after him."

"Men . . . robes," Stephen said. "One had a knife at my stomach."

The other M.P., tall and balding, recognized Alexei from the base. "You're the Nagavatsky kid—your father's the dog man, right? What's your name?"

"Alexei."

"It's an old Packard station wagon," Stephen said. "They tried to pull me into it. . . . I ripped one of their robes. . . ."

The M.P.s listened. Stephen noticed them exchanging a look. "You think we're making this up." He could feel his face flush, and he shifted his weight from one foot to the other. "You don't believe us, do you?"

The other M.P. pointed behind the boys. "Monks, like *them*?"

Stephen and Alexei turned. There, emerging from a church, was a tour group of monks, all in robes and hoods. Another cluster of robed men was watching an Indian rain dance.

"Hey, we'll take a report," the tall M.P. said. He put one hand on Stephen's shoulder. "We believe you. Did you see what they looked like? Their faces?"

"No." Stephen shook off the M.P.'s hand.

The short M.P. got a pad out and started jotting things down. Stephen told them everything he knew. Everything from the moment he'd gotten to town. *At least four men, some with accents. The Packard. Monks . . .*

The M.P.s said they were going to call his father. They'd talk to him. Stephen began to regret he'd said anything. "Where and when are you supposed to meet up again with the Los Alamos bus?"

"Four o'clock in front of the Cristo Rey Church. My teacher's name is Mrs. Haines," Stephen said.

Alexei pulled him aside. "We're getting out of here—I've got my dad's truck. You'll be safer back at the base than waiting around here."

Stephen and Alexei remained polite and respectful, and even got the M.P.s to get the word to Mrs. Haines and the bus driver so nobody'd be worried that a scientist's son was missing. When the M.P.s had finished grilling Stephen and Alexei, they escorted them to Alexei's truck. Once they got in, Alexei burned rubber, leaving the M.P.s in the dust.

"What if the monks try to follow us?" Stephen said, turning in his seat.

"No old Packard's going to catch this rig," Alexei said. "No way."

The traffic was light traveling away from Santa Fe. But on the approach to the main security gate, the cars and military trucks were bumper to bumper. Alexei parked at the holding lot, and then he and Stephen hiked the rest of the way up to pass through the security check.

As they started walking down the main street past the rows of green clapboard buildings, there were more personnel than usual. A WAC came running past them, tears on her face.

"What happened?" Stephen asked.

The WAC mumbled something, but neither Stephen nor Alexei got it. They stopped Giulio, one of the Fermi kids.

"What's the matter?" Alexei asked.

Giulio didn't answer.

Other men and women looked frozen or stunned, not knowing which way to turn. A crowd was fast forming outside the main offices. Oppenheimer came out on the steps. He began to speak to the gathering.

Solemnly.

The words were about grieving and the loss and death of a national leader.

"What is he saying?" Alexei asked.

"Roosevelt's dead," Stephen said. "That's what he's saying. He's said the President of the United States died today."

President Roosevelt is dead. Impossible words pouring out of the head physicist's mouth.

There would be a Sunday memorial. . . . Everyone, in and out of the Tech Area, would be able to attend. . . .

Many grown men and women in the crowd were crying now. Construction men. Men and women in uniform. Tears were on their faces. One woman collapsed in shock.

Stephen heard prayers as Oppenheimer continued to speak from his heart: We who are unaccustomed to tears should cry. We who are looking with deep trouble to the future and our dream of ending this terrible war should take care. As we remember how our President has helped us live through these years of great evil and of great terror, let us be reminded of how precious and rare a thing human greatness is. Our President had been our guide, our Commander-in-Chief, and in an old and truest sense—our leader. We pray that his spirit and intent will continue, that the great horror of our time will come to a conclusion and not be repeated. We ask for the strength to remember that man is a creature whose substance is faith. . . .

We do not know if our project will continue. We all must feel less certain that our efforts will come to a good end. . . .

Sewa opened the front door of the house at Bathtub Row.

"Alexei's staying for dinner," Stephen told her after Alexei had gone inside. "He's my friend and he's welcome to come over to see me whenever he wants."

Sewa was quiet.

Her eyes locked on Alexei as Stephen went into the bathroom and closed the door.

The death of President Roosevelt had shaken Stephen and awakened in him, once more, the terror of the men in hoods after him. He would make certain that Sewa and his dad knew Alexei had saved him. He'd tell them about the chase and the knife at his stomach. As the reality of what the men had done, their stalking him and trying to force him into a car, socked into him, he felt a mixture of rage and humiliation.

Alone in the bathroom, he let the water from the tap run hot onto a washcloth. He pressed and re-pressed the warmth onto his face and waited for his tears to stop.

Dr. Orr came home late and exhausted. Sewa served him and the boys a turkey-and-vegetable pie with potatoes that had been baked in corn husks. As they sat around the table eating, it was clear the M.P.s hadn't reported anything to him yet. Stephen told about the men dressed as monks. The men who had followed him from the post office, and . . .

I told you you shouldn't go to town. I didn't want you to go. You shouldn't have been alone.

Stephen told enough so his father and Sewa would understand that Alexei had saved him. He left out the stark dread and fright of it. The parts that made him nauseated. If he let them see that, he knew, he'd never get out of the house alone again.

His father and Sewa listened silently.

When Stephen had finished, his father asked a few questions, got up from the table, and went to the hall phone. Stephen knew his father was dialing Security to find out about any reports the M.P.s had filed. His father spoke quietly into the phone. After a few minutes Stephen heard him chuckle.

Good.

Stephen guessed the M.P.s were making light of everything. *Oh, yes, your son told us about it. Your son and the dog man's kid.*

Monks.

Monks chasing them.

His dad's face was serious again when he came back to the table. "One of the M.P.s remembered seeing a Packard like the one you described," he said.

Stephen and Alexei kept eating.

"I'm glad you were there to help Stephen," his father told Alexei. "You're a good friend. Even if this was some kind of a prank, a few jokers who'd had a little too much to drink, you both have to be more careful. Off base and on base."

"We will," Alexei said.

"Right, Dad."

Sewa got Dr. Orr a cup of coffee. He had more to say over the dessert of strawberry ice cream and gooseberries. "I was late because of a meeting. Alexei's father was there. Harry Truman succeeds Roosevelt as President of the United States. He's a straight shooter from Missouri. He's already called Oppie."

"Is the project over?" Stephen asked.

Dr. Orr hesitated. He looked at Alexei, then at Stephen. "No."

After dinner Dr. Orr excused himself and turned in for the night. Alexei went home, and Stephen offered to help Sewa with the dishes in the kitchen.

"You still don't like Alexei, do you?" he said. "He saved my life, and you still don't like him."

Sewa said nothing. She tossed him a drying towel.

"Those 'monks' almost had me. They would have slit my throat if it wasn't for Alexei."

"I know you believe that," Sewa said.

"You're beating around the bush again and trying to make everything about Alexei suspicious and mixed up. I don't know why," Stephen said. "What's eating you?"

Sewa rinsed the silverware under the faucet. "You know, my father was a good hunter," she said. "He was very cunning. He knew many tricks."

"What are you talking about?"

"I remember one hunting trick," Sewa said. "It's called the trick of deadly disguise. My father told me how hunters would wear a fresh wolf's skin to crawl into the edge of a buffalo herd." She brushed her hair away from her eyes. "Buffalo are not afraid of wolves, so a skillful archer wearing a wolf's skin can kill seven— eight!—animals before the herd catches on and stampedes."

"So you think that's what the monks were all about? Is that what you're saying? They're like Alexei's wolf's skin so we'll let him hang around our house? A deadly disguise the Nagavatskys cooked up? You're saying Alexei's a spy!"

"No . . ."

"Yes, you are," Stephen said. "You think it's all a big setup and I'm being fooled."

May 1

Dear Mom,

I hope you're laying off the horsemeat. I don't want to make you worry about me, but I'm feeling very alone. I don't seem to be able to talk to Dad anymore. He tells me I ask too many questions. I know he told you about what happened in Santa Fe. He said that should have been enough to make me stop asking questions. I don't know how to say it. He seems crazy. It's like he's in some other world. It's getting so that I really wish I had stayed in London with you.

I'm writing this letter at the desk in my room. It's in front of a big window, and it's nine o'clock. I often end up alone at night. The whole sky in New Mexico is mobbed with stars. I usually work on my models and war journal. All the articles I have for my journal are about people killing each other. Grown-ups killing each other. Killing women and children. It's really nuts. Sometimes, in the middle of everything, I remember Jackson and feel so mad and scared, I don't know what to do.

I feel better when I'm at my friend Alexei's ranch. Alexei has a nice family. When I'm with them, I remember how we used to be. Mr. Nagavatsky is a good cook. The only thing I don't like is that once in a while he barbecues an armadillo. He was born in a city in Russia where they eat a lot of different things. He tells us stories around the campfire and says things like "War is death's feast."

Dad hasn't noticed, but I'm trying to grow a mustache. I don't think he'd notice if I grew another head. More later. Write to me as soon as possible.

Love,
Stephen

P.S. Sewa's really getting on my nerves. She hates all the Nagavatskys.

12

Two Months to Deadline

Stephen was in his room when the words shot out at him from the radio: *"Adolf Hitler has committed suicide. . . ."*

"Hitler is dead!" he heard Sewa shouting from the kitchen. "He's dead!"

"I heard it!" Stephen called back. He began jotting down snippets of the news report in his journal as the announcer gave more details: *"Hitler killed himself after two other Third Reich generals took control of the German army. The generals are negotiating an unconditional surrender with the combined chiefs and U.S.*

General Eisenhower. . . ."

Stephen wanted to speak to his father, but he was still working in the Tech Area. *Now* maybe the project would be over.

Stephen decided he'd go see Alexei. *His* father would be home. Mr. Nagavatsky would be close by, at least. A family, where everybody talked and shared things. He grabbed his jacket and headed out the door.

"Where are you going?" Sewa called after him.

"Guess," Stephen said.

He cut across a muddy street toward the perimeter fence behind the school, the stretch of chain-link fence not patrolled by dogs. There was no military guard in sight as he lifted the bottom of the fence and stooped under it. He knew he could circle east from the stables to the Rio Grande and follow the river the two miles to Alexei's ranch.

From a butte called Dead Horse Point he caught sight of the gash in the mesa below San Ildefonso. He followed the jagged edge of the gorge, then broke into a run. Beyond a field of nightshade were the railroad bridge and the ranch. He kept clear of the main kennel runs. A few of the dogs were in the outside runs. They remembered him and came, wagging their tails, to the edge of the fence.

Stephen ran up on the sprawling porch of the main house. The door was closed. He knocked on it and cupped his hands to see in through the small, dusty window. The glass eyes of a stuffed elk head stared back at him from the dining-room wall. In the shadows he could see Mr. Nagavatsky's fur wall hangings.

He knocked again. No one. Stephen knew someone would come back soon. Alexei. Mr. Nagavatsky. Aunt Ludmila or one of the ranch hands. He shielded his eyes from the sun and looked up toward the litter shed.

"Lady's had a new batch of puppies," Alexei had told him a few days before.

"Can I see them?" Stephen had asked.

"Sure. When she's not feeding, we'll bring a few of them down."

Stephen decided to stroll up the rise toward the shed, hoping he would catch a glimpse of the litter. Closer, he noticed the shed had its own fencing around it. From one side of the shed, he could see all the way to the bottom of the gorge with its thin snake of a river.

It made him dizzy.

He moved away from the gorge, climbed a foot or so up the fence, and tried to see in through one of the shed windows. A shadow moved behind the glass. Behind the shade . . . Something.

It might be the wind. A door opened. He was holding tight to the top of the fence, both feet hooked into the wire like boots into a pair of stirrups. Something was moving toward him.

A dark shape.

Fast.

A large animal, shredding dirt with its paws, and then airborne. The dog crashed into the fence, jaws trying to bite through to his face. Stephen let go and fell backward. He found himself near the edge of the abyss, with the dog barking.

Snarling.

Stephen was on his knees, then standing and running back down toward the ranch house.

His mouth was warm with blood where he'd bitten his own lip. He didn't understand. There were supposed to be puppies. Puppies and a mother. Instead he was attacked by a lone male dog.

In the distance there was a dust cloud. A truck was coming. He knew it would be Mr. Nagavatsky and Alexei. He didn't want them to know he had been up to the litter shed.

Nosey.

He dusted himself off.

Mr. Nagavatsky and Alexei pulled up. Alexei got out of the truck. "Germany's surrendering! The Nazis gave up." Alexei was speaking quickly, the words running together. "Hitler committed suicide . . ."

"Yes," Stephen said. "That's why I came over."

Mr. Nagavatsky said, "Eisenhower was on the radio just now."

"Everybody at Los Alamos is celebrating," Alexei said. "The scientists are in the street drinking champagne. There's a big party. Oppie and Groves put on a show. Everyone's dancing in the street."

"My father?" Stephen asked. "Was he cele-brating, too? Did you see him?"

Alexei threw his mane of raven hair behind him. "No, I didn't see him."

"Your dad wasn't there," Mr. Nagavatsky said.

The victory celebration was still in full swing by the time Stephen got back to the base. There was music. A makeshift dance floor had been cleared in front of the commissary. A group of the scientists had put together a band of drums, piano, and a couple of clarinets. The wife of Dr. Bradford, a British physicist, was at a mike from the rec hall, leading the singing.

> "... There _are_ bluebirds over
> The white cliffs of Dover ..."

Metal folding tables had been set up and covered with cream cakes, steaming casseroles, and cold-cut sandwiches. The back of a supply truck had been converted into a bar with red wine and pitchers of spiked fruit juices. M.P.s posted at beer kegs filled up mugs and passed them out to the WACs and soldiers.

Stephen grabbed a bottle of Coke. He spotted Oppenheimer and Bainbridge, General Groves, and lots of the other physicists and techs with their families. He went up to them.

"Have you seen my dad?"

"I thought he was around," Bainbridge said.

Stephen didn't see him.

Stephen hadn't seen people having such a good time since one of his father's brothers had gotten married. One of his uncles had danced a jig, and his grandmother, as usual, had sung "A Good Man Is Hard to Find" and "My Blue Heaven."

There was a table piled high with pies and cakes. Stephen wolfed down a rice pudding and stuffed a chocolate chip cookie into his pocket. He slid a charlotte russe onto a plate and headed for Bathtub Row.

"Roll out the barrel,
We'll have a barrel of fun . . ."

Stephen sang along with a couple of privates who were dancing a polka in front of the barber shop. Lights were burning in every window of the Sundts and Quonset huts. Doors were wide open and casement windows were cranked wide. A square dance had started on one of the lawns.

Stephen turned into Bathtub Row. He wondered how much longer it would be before Japan surrendered, too—until Oppenheimer would announce that they were closing the base. They wouldn't need Los Alamos. Or his father. The secret could end.

"No more school, no more books . . ."

He broke into a jog. His mother would be coming back. His father would teach again at Berkeley or North Carolina or someplace. He thought of Alexei. Stephen and he would get together every year; he'd visit Alexei wherever the Nagavatskys were.

Stephen didn't see any M.P.s when he

unlocked the door to the house and went inside. It was dark. He turned on a lamp in the living room. There was a strip of light beneath the door to his father's room. He ran down the hall and flung open the door.

His father was sitting at his desk in front of a map stuck with flag pins. A map of greens and gold, with squiggly lines for roads and railroad tracks crossing each other like twisted bundles of nerves. Thick reports and files were spread out on top of his bed.

"Dad, why aren't you . . . ?"

As Stephen ran to his father, he remembered he should have knocked. His father had told him he must. But he had brought the charlotte russe with its whipped cream, and there was the celebration outside.

His father shifted to block the view of his desk, but Stephen had seen the chart of Japan, its crescent of islands and intricate bays surrounded by ocean. The needle flags were stuck in like pins in a pincushion.

Flags on the largest cities.

"Germany's surrendering. It's over," Stephen

said as he held the charlotte russe out. "It's over."

His father turned suddenly in his chair, one of his arms swinging toward Stephen and knocking him and the plate onto the floor.

"It's *not* over," he heard his father say.

Stephen froze. His instincts told him not to move. Not to breathe. But he tried to get up. He'd get up and leave the room, he told himself. Next time he'd knock.

"Don't move. You'll cut yourself."

His father's voice was softer now. Recognizable.

"But everyone says it's as good as over," Stephen said. "The war—"

"They're wrong."

His father kneeled on the floor next to him and started picking up the broken pieces of plate.

"Everyone says the Japanese are going to surrender," Stephen said. "They'll give up, like the Germans."

His father's arm was around him now as he sat on the floor.

"You don't understand, Stephen," his father said.

"What?"

"There are things you don't have to know."

Stephen looked at his father's gaunt and hunched figure. "Dad, let me decide what I have to know."

"We've been fighting two wars. We knew months ago the Germans were going to surrender. Their troops were camped next to our Allied troops. Both sides had been sharing food for a long time. Even playing cards together. Neither side has fired a shot in weeks. Both sides were hoping someone would get rid of Hitler. Finally, he did everyone a favor and put a bullet into his own brain. Then, and only then, were the Germans allowed to surrender."

"So the Japanese will surrender, too."

"Stephen, the Japanese will *never* surrender. The Japanese have been ordered not to stop fighting until they eat stones. Until they're all dead and lying facedown in the dirt. That's what their emperor has ordered them to do. Hirohito's a Japanese Hitler."

"So they'll get tired, they'll get tired of dying," Stephen said.

"No. Even when they're wounded—taking their last breath—they try to kill us. Or they hide grenades on themselves and hope to slaughter us from their graves."

A drunk private on a bike rode by out on the street. His voice shot in through the window of the room: *"We whacked the Krauts! We whacked 'em good."*

Stephen's father closed the shutters and shut the window.

"Hirohito has everyone brainwashed to commit hara-kiri. They strap themselves into kamikaze airplanes. When we took the Japanese island of Saipan, whole villages of people jumped off thousand-foot-high sea cliffs to their deaths on the jagged rocks below. Entire Japanese families. Some were pushed or were ordered by Japanese officers to jump—all to avoid the shame and terror of being captured by us. How do you fight a people like that?

"If you really want to know the secret of Los Alamos, this is all you have to know. If we win the race here, we are going to save a half a million, maybe a million American lives—and who knows how many others' lives. That's all of the secret you need to understand."

Stephen's father tossed the last pieces of the broken plate into the wastepaper basket. "There are forces beyond your control. Beyond mine. Things that nobody can stop. Certainly not you or I."

Stephen stood up. "I'm sorry I barged in," he said. He started out, but there was one thing more he wanted to say. He felt like telling his dad that he'd seen Soifer. That he knew the secret was something unspeakable. Instead, he said nothing and went to his room.

14

June 16, 1945
One Month to Deadline

Alexei was waiting for Stephen when he got out of class on Friday. "Soifer's being moved," he said.

"How do you know?" Stephen asked.

"The orderlies told me. They're shipping him home tomorrow to die."

"I want to see him again," Stephen said. "Who's on duty tonight?"

"Klass."

"Dr. Soifer's the only one who ever told us anything. Maybe he'd tell us more about the 'Tail of the Tiger.' All the experiments. He'd probably tell us exactly what they're making now. There's got to be a way in."

"There is—the horses. Last October, Jason had chicken pox and was quarantined for a week," Alexei said. "The Barbarian wouldn't let me in to see him, so I saddled up Crazy and rode him around to the back of the hospital. I went in through a window. We played gin rummy for hours."

"What about the M.P.s?"

"If they see a horse, all they want to do is pet it. They're suckers for Crazy and Smally. We can do it, but it's got to be tonight or Soifer's going to be gone."

Alexei stayed for dinner at Bathtub Row. Dr. Orr was working late. Sewa looked suspicious when Stephen told her he and Alexei were going to play basketball down at the rec center.

"Your father wants you back before ten," Sewa reminded Stephen.

"Sure."

By eight, Stephen and Alexei had the horses saddled and had ridden them around to the main entrance gate. Alexei knew the M.P.s. They waved them through.

"Follow me," Alexei said.

He rode Crazy down the main street as far as the darkened laundry and south wing of the hospital grounds. They loped across a lawn right up to the window of Soifer's room.

"You go in," Alexei said, taking Smally's reins. "He only talks to you anyway. I'll stay with the horses."

Stephen pushed open the shutters. Looking through the half-open window, he saw Dr. Soifer, barely recognizable, lying in his bed. The several tubes that hung down from the intravenous stand made him look like a frail, ghastly puppet. Stephen passed the reins to Alexei, opened the window wide, and slid into the room.

Soifer looked at him.

"Hello, Dr. Soifer," Stephen said. "Do you remember me? Olaf's son."

Soifer's lips trembled. In a weak, appalling voice, he said, "Help me lift my head. Oh, God, I have to change my position. Help me. . . ."

Stephen went to his bedside, let down the aluminum rail from the side of the bed, and slid a pillow beneath Soifer's head. Dr. Soifer's face looked white and dead. His red, wet eyes stayed locked on Stephen.

"How are you?" Stephen asked.

"How am I?"

"Yes."

"I'm dying from the inside out. The radiation is rotting my body." Soifer nodded toward the bed stand.

Stephen filled a drinking glass from the pitcher of ice water. He lifted the glass to Dr. Soifer's lips.

"What do you want, Olaf's son?" Soifer asked as he sipped the water. Stephen realized Soifer's mind was still working. That he had memory and thought and was still smart.

"The Gadget," Stephen said. "I need to know . . . what is it? *Exactly*. I want to know—"

"It is . . . the sun."

"What do you mean, *it's the sun*?"

"A sun that might burn the whole sky. The atmosphere itself may catch fire. We don't know." Soifer looked away to the sounds of the horses at the window. "What we're making will be like a tornado. An unbelievable . . . light. . . .Thousands of people will die." Dr. Soifer reached out and grasped Stephen's arm. "Some will feel as though they have been struck in the back by a hammer. Others will become small black bundles. Even if they know it is coming . . . even if children hide—it won't matter. Everyone will be screaming. Those who live will be walking dazed through the streets, dragging their skins behind them. That is what the Gadget is. . . ."

Stephen heard the sound of voices coming down the hall. They were close, almost at the room. Quickly he lifted the aluminum rail back into place and hid behind the open door. He heard Alexei moving the horses away from the window. Nurse Klass and two Indian orderlies came into the room.

Stephen held his breath as they talked and moved Dr. Soifer onto a gurney. They were talking about a restaurant up in Taos—and an adobe house in Ranchos de Taos. Then Klass turned the conversation to a discussion of Bette Davis in the movie *Watch on the Rhine*.

15

July 1, 1945
Two Weeks to Deadline

Both boys were convinced something was going to happen soon.

At the beginning of July Alexei asked to stay over nearly every night at Bathtub Row. Stephen's father said it could only be on weekends. By the second weekend Stephen and Alexei had noticed an increase in the number of trucks leaving the base at night. Sometimes they were regulation troop trucks and vans, but other times, at three or four in the morning, there were armed soldiers in jeeps escorting flatbeds carrying huge, canvas-draped shapes.

"Something's happening," Stephen said.

"I think so too," Alexei said.

When Stephen was at the PX, he heard the pharmacist complaining to an assistant that they were running out of aspirin and sleeping pills. In the dining hall the physicists spoke at a rapid, whispered clip.

There was a tension creeping into everyone and everything, like the nagging ticking of a loud clock.

In the first week of July Stephen's father told him his work would take him off base and he'd be away for a few days. Oppenheimer and Groves needed him, and he had to go. Sewa would stay full-time at Bathtub Row and take care of him.

"I understand, Dad," Stephen said.

"Good," his father said.

One night a truck left with what looked like two enormous airplane wings hidden beneath canvas drapes.

"I think it really is a plane," Stephen told Alexei. "Maybe it flies faster or uses radiation for fuel."

"I think it's a plane too," Alexei said.

"They probably need to test it where no spies or anyone can see it. An airport in Arizona . . ."

"No," Alexei said in the shadows of Stephen's bedroom. "They're going south. A couple of hundred miles or so."

"How could you know?"

Alexei hesitated.

"My father was in Albuquerque," he said. "He was talking with Apaches who work down there in a feed store. On weekends some of them go out and collect turquoise in the desert. They said they heard machine-gun fire."

. "Machine-gun fire?"

"Soldiers were hunting antelope with machine guns. The Indians said there were a lot of other soldiers and trucks. The Jornada del Muerto Desert. That's where they are going to test whatever they are testing. There are dry lake beds all over there. A really big plane could take off from there. It's *now*, Stephen. Everything we've been wanting to know. We've got to go down and see it! Let's find out what the big secret is once and for all."

"Yes," Stephen said. "I want to go."

Sunday morning Stephen's dad woke him up to say good-bye. His father's hands were trembling with nerves as he held a cup of coffee.

"Don't worry about me," Stephen said.

After his father left, Stephen told Sewa he would be going to stay at Alexei's for the night. She wouldn't have to worry about him. There was going to be a cookout, and Mr. Nagavatsky said he would take them swimming in the Rio Grande.

"I think you should stay here," Sewa said. "This is a very important time."

"What are you talking about?"

"I think you know."

Stephen smiled. He asked her to make an extra batch of almond pralines and squash cookies for him to take with him in case Mr. Nagavatsky would be barbecuing anything he didn't like.

"You'll have to sift the flour for the cookies," Sewa said.

"It's a deal."

"Is Mr. Nagavatsky picking you up?" Sewa wanted to know.

"Yes," Stephen lied.

Stephen grabbed a canteen, a heavy pullover in case the temperature dropped at night, and a pair of his father's binoculars. For a moment he thought he wouldn't take the binoculars, but he decided he might need them. He was about to head out of his room when he remembered the dark "sunglasses" Dr. Soifer had given him.

He got them out of his desk and put them into his backpack. He said good-bye to Sewa and started toward the main gate. There were twice as many guards checking everyone and every vehicle coming onto the base and leaving it.

Stephen was glad to see a familiar face.

"Hey, Mitchell," Stephen said.

The M.P. looked at him. "Oh, yeah. Hi, Stephen." Mitchell had gotten used to Mr. Nagavatsky coming to pick Stephen up. "The truck's over there."

"Thanks," Stephen said. He flashed his regular pass anyway and ran down to the turnaround. The mountains were burning red in the setting sun.

Alexei was waiting in his dad's pickup. Stephen opened the door and swung up into the passenger seat.

"We're off," Alexei said.

They hit the steep and narrow switchbacks and passed the San Ildefonso pueblo. It was dark by the time they got through Santa Fe and picked up the main highway south.

There was a waxing half moon and a storm of stars in the sky. Stephen got Alexei to play word games to kill time. South of Albuquerque they trailed a Dixie bus for a while, whistling and waving at a couple of girls who waved back at them from the rear window. Alexei got Stephen to sing songs.

*"A hundred bottles of beer of the wall,
A hundred bottles of beer . . ."*

It was close to midnight when they passed near Jornada del Muerto. The headlights picked up turns and skid marks on the side of the road.

"Go farther," Stephen said. "There'll be guards, M.P.s, watching everything that moves on the roads. They've got to have tanks, maybe helicopters."

"We can take one of the old mine roads."

"Good."

"There are lava beds and badlands."

When they finally turned, a vast stretch of moonlit wasteland lay before them. Black clouds were moving off the mountains on the night horizon.

"Why is the sand so white?" Stephen asked.

"Gypsum," Alexei said. "It's in the ground all over here. Lots of cement companies dig it up."

A fog had begun to rise and drift through the lava beds. Soon a light rain was falling.

"Good," Alexei said, switching to the truck's fog lights. "It won't be easy to spot us. This is the Army's main firing range in New Mexico, even though there are cliff dwellings in the mountains. "

Stephen began to wonder how Alexei would know so many details about where they were. Why hadn't he mentioned any of it before? "How do you know?" Stephen asked.

Alexei parked the pickup at the edge of a stream. He shut the motor and fog lights off. "I was down here a few times with my dad when they needed guard dogs. They'd have a new gun or plane they were testing, and they wanted the dogs in the hangars with them around the clock." Alexei reached around and lifted the cover on the cab's storage compartment. He pulled out a couple of sleeping bags and tossed one at Stephen.

"Thanks," Stephen said. He scrunched up one end of it into a pillow and snuggled back.

"The fog is thick," Alexei said.

"In England, when there was a fog, my cousin Jackson and I used to stay up late and tell ghost stories," Stephen said.

"Like what?"

"One was about some man who had lost a hand and had a metal hook instead. If you were in London, you were supposed to be really careful when you walked in the fog, because this man would find you and whack you on the side of the head. He'd drive his hook into your brain."

"Nice," Alexei said, staring out the front window as the fog closed in around the truck.

"What's the most horrible story you ever heard?" Stephen asked.

Alexei shivered. "My father told me that when he was a kid in Russia, his mother got him to come home every night by telling him that there were goatsuckers that would come out of the forest. A lot of the kids said it was true. They had seen goatsuckers. They said a goatsucker had four-foot leather wings, the legs of a bull, and a head like a human skull. And it had the stink of a corpse, that's what everyone said. It would sink its fangs into a kid's throat and drain the blood out."

"That's horrible," Stephen said.

Finally both of them drifted off to sleep.

When Stephen woke up, he didn't know if it was the sounds outside the pickup or the first glow of dawn that had disturbed him. He looked at his watch. It was a few minutes after five in the morning. Alexei was still sleeping behind the wheel of the pickup.

Stephen nudged Alexei.

"What?" Alexei asked as he swung his feet down from the dashboard.

"Listen."

At first Alexei said he didn't hear anything, but then the sounds got louder.

A scratching.

Stephen rolled down his window. Three large deer were feeding on scrub bushes next to the truck. At the sound of the window opening, they bolted across an open field and disappeared down into an arroyo. Stephen was surprised at the crashing their hooves made on the earth, a pounding that shook the ground and could be felt in the truck.

Alexei opened his door and dropped down to the ground. He grabbed a thermos out of his backpack and took a drink of orange juice.

Stephen was already breaking out Sewa's pralines. He stuffed a few into his pockets and got out of the truck.

Alexei led the way south several hundred feet along the stream, to a point where it narrowed at the lava beds and a natural footbridge allowed them to cross easily. The water was deeper here, rushing, becoming white water on the bed of rocks. The rain clouds and fog had passed over.

Stephen and Alexei started the trek up the steep slope that led to the cusp of the flats. The rising sun played tricks with Stephen's eyes, making stones and arroyos appear to move.

"I think it's got to be a flying wing. Six engines. No fuselage," Alexei said. "It's probably as big as a football field."

"It could be a new helicopter," Stephen said.

Alexei signaled Stephen to slow down and hunch over as they reached the top of the ridge. They lay down to check out the vast flat valley below. Stephen grabbed the binoculars out of his backpack.

"What do you see?" Alexei said.

"There's a row of . . ." Stephen hesitated, trying to decide exactly what he was seeing in the distance. "They look like bunkers."

The sun was rising fast. "Let me see," Alexei said, taking the binoculars. He swung them to look toward a cluster of lights at the south of the flats. "They've got the base camp down there. It's at least a couple of miles away. I see tents and barracks."

"Can you see any plane?"

"No."

Stephen took the binoculars back. He let out a yelp as something scooted past him.

"It's only a horned toad," Alexei said, throwing a pebble to scare the lizard away.

Stephen swung the binoculars in a slow sweep from the south of the desert valley to the north. He stopped at something dead center. It took him a moment to refocus and find what had caught his eye. "There's a tower. Why's a tower in the middle of the flats?"

Suddenly whole banks of flood lamps were blazing at the base camp.

"What's happening?" Alexei asked.

Stephen passed the binoculars to Alexei. He focused them on the camp. "I can see Oppenheimer in his porkpie hat."

"What's he doing?"

"Heading into one of the bunkers. It looks like there's a lot of guards with big cameras."

A loud voice began to reverberate off the rim of the valley.

"What's that?"

"Loudspeakers," Alexei said. "They've got loudspeakers all over the place." He swung the binoculars south to the barracks. "The soldiers have dropped down. They're on their stomachs, putting on goggles or something."

Somewhere an amplified gong had been sounded, along with buzzers, terrible piercing noises. Now Stephen's ears were used to the voice from the loudspeakers. He understood what the voice was saying:

"NINE . . . EIGHT . . . SEVEN . . ."

Someone counting.

Counting while everyone had slipped into bunkers or lain down in trenches. Stephen found himself reaching into his backpack and taking out the sunglasses.

"SIX . . . FIVE . . ."

Rockets were in the sky. Red. Green. Flares.

Stephen swung the binoculars back to the tower. It was black and steel, with immense concrete footings and metal cross struts.

A high platform of corrugated iron . . .

"It's not a plane," Stephen shouted. "Run! It's a . . ."

Alexei had already turned. He was ahead of Stephen racing back down the hill toward the stream. The final numbers echoed in Stephen's ears:

"THREE . . . TWO . . . ONE . . ."

In the last second Alexei reached the stream and dove into the water. Stephen had ten feet more to travel when the whole of his world became a brilliant, scalding flash. Stephen was bathed in a searing brightness as he put on the sunglasses. When he turned, he saw a ball of fire on the horizon. Huge. It expanded. In front of it rolled a thick skirt of lumpy matter.

The light bored its way straight through to Stephen's bones. He felt the light with his whole body, as the enormous ball of fire grew and rolled and swelled.

It began to rise in the air, twisting like a left-handed screw. Stephen dove into the stream. He tried to go deep, as deep as he could. Stephen's eyes burned. He pulled himself deeper still. The current dragged him over the sharp bottom rocks, slamming him, scraping him. His lungs began to hurt, and he felt as if they would rupture.

Time stood still as he fought his way back up to the surface. When he hit the air, he was tossed against the lava rocks. The steep sides of the stream scraped his arms as he tried to get a hold. When he was certain he would die, he was washed into a pool that had been eroded in the side of the bank.

A sheltered basin.

Choking, he stood in the pool and looked at the sky. Now the fire was a mile high. Still twisting.

Higher still.

He began to cry. Crying as the giant fireball scorched the heavens and the earth for miles. The earth looked on fire. Then he saw Alexei, wheezing, clinging to a rock at the water's edge.

17

Stephen helped Alexei to his feet and up onto the bank of the stream. They were dazed beneath the column of fire and smoke as it pierced a heaven of clouds. There was a shuffling in the sands and on the lava rock. Men silhouetted against the fireball of the bomb surrounded them.

CLICK. CLICK.

Gun triggers were set and ready, rifles swung up onto the shoulders of uniformed men and pointed at them. Stephen waited to be shot. Instead, a voice shouted a signal, and a handful of men charged forward.

Alexei was half carried in one direction, Stephen in the other. Pain radiated down the side of Stephen's face. It was as if he had been in a devastating car crash. Quickly—in his wet clothes—he was wedged between two soldiers in the back of an Army van.

Stephen didn't know what they were talking about, didn't care as the van raced toward the base camp. They stopped at a strange-looking shed, and he was rushed inside. Geiger counters clicked as he let the medics strip him. He found himself under the pounding spray from a shower nozzle.

"Put these on, put on the clothes . . ."

Two medics were going over him, checking his eyes and face and arms. He was in an Army shirt and pants and dry shoes that were too big for him. He felt lost. He bumped into the edge of a table. "Where's Alexei?" Stephen asked.

He was aware of the men talking to him, asking question after question. His sides were hurting as though he'd been kicked. He had been moved to a bunker now, a cement room with narrow slits for windows. A male nurse was treating the scrapes on his legs and arms.

Then his father was in the room.

His father talking fast. Angry and frustrated. Surprised. Asking too many questions that Stephen's mind couldn't find words to answer. His father looked outraged and embarrassed. Too busy to deal with it. With the trespassing. *I didn't mean anything,* Stephen thought about saying. He tried to get the words out. I wanted to see the plane, the new plane, the flying wing . . . Alexei and I wanted to know the secret. . . .

But he couldn't stop his eyes from closing. For a few moments more he heard his father's voice. More questions. Whispering.

Furious.

Stephen escaped into sleep. When he awoke, it was night and he was in the back of a speeding jeep. A draft sliced in at him through the cracked and warped Plexiglas windows. An M.P. was at the wheel.

Stephen's father sat next to the M.P. For a moment he turned and looked back at Stephen and their eyes locked. His father looked chilled, alarmed—staring at him with a face gripped by fear. Some man's voice was on the jeep radio. Bing Crosby or someone with Tommy Dorsey's band. Singing a silly song: "Mairsy Doats and Dosie Doats . . ."

No one in the jeep speaking. Stephen couldn't forget the piece of the sun swelling. The shock wave and spire of burning gases.

When the jeep arrived back at Los Alamos, there were smiles. The M.P.s at Security applauded his father. People already knew the project was a success. They were waving. His father waved back.

Stephen got out of the jeep and headed down the front walk. Sewa was waiting in the open doorway. She knew everything. She spoke to his father for a few minutes while Stephen changed out of the Army clothes and into his other shoes and a pair of fresh jeans. Then Sewa came in with white salve and pressed it gently on his scrapes. The cream was cool. He lay on the bed with his head propped up against pillows.

"I made beef and creamed eggplant," Sewa said. "There are more pralines, too." She had made up plates, and they would be waiting for him and his father when they were hungry. She asked nothing about what he'd seen. Nothing about what he'd done. Or what had happened.

She didn't ask about Alexei.

A letter had come from his mother, and she left it with him to read in the silence of his room:

St. James Infirmary, London
July 12, 1945

My dearest son, Stephen,
There is so much to tell you. Your cousins David and Sean ask about you. Molly still sings "G.I. Jive" at the drop of a hat. She asks about you too. I think she's finally accepted that her brother will not be coming back. I suppose we've all accepted it by now.

I've been working at the hospital here. There are many Londoners who are still in great pain from the last of the rocket attacks. Men and women, even babies, are brought in for continued treatment. A lot of them have lost a limb or have terrible burn scars.

On Saturdays I try to go to the park, the one you and I always went to . . . where you'd feed the ducks and pigeons. A band plays every Saturday, lots of old English songs and waltzes. Some of the men and women are on crutches, but they still want to dance. It brings tears to my eyes when I hear the music and see them. Yes, I suppose we're all coming back together as a country.

I'll be able to leave London soon, Stephen, and I will come to New Mexico. I'll write as soon as I know the exact date. I promise to make you a rib roast. We'll have our next Thanksgiving with turkey and cranberries. We'll go out in a party boat and fish for porgies.

We'll be a family again, like everyone. Soon, Stephen. Remember us.

Love,
Mom

Stephen rested his head back against the pillows. He wouldn't think about anything he shouldn't. A couple of months would go by, and all the things his mother had written about would come true. He'd be silent. That would be better for everyone.

His journal lay on his desk in the corner. It was thick, neatly pasted up. Everything in order. The models of battleships sat neatly on bases of polished wood. The B-17 Flying Fortress, Spitfire, and P-38 hung from the rafter with several other planes. They turned slowly in a draft.

His father was in the doorway.

"You won't tell anyone what you saw," his father said—coldly—matter-of-factly.

Stephen stared at his father, standing there in his faded plaid bathrobe and leather slippers. Stephen tried not to say anything, but he couldn't help himself.

"You're going to drop bombs on the cities, aren't you?" Stephen said. "Cities you were sticking pins into on your map. How many innocent people are you going to kill?"

"Some of them aren't so innocent," his father said. "We have seen other Japanese cities that we have bombed. There are always heavy-duty drill presses and huge guns being assembled in most of the homes. They stick up through the roofs, wreckage. The Japanese don't have factories like the Germans for us to bomb. Their whole country builds their airplanes and tanks in their homes."

"You could set one of the bombs off in the ocean, blow it up where all Tokyo could see it. You don't need to drop a bomb like that on a city. They'd surrender if they saw it. If they just knew we had it."

"We don't know that."

"But you could try."

"Stephen, you should stop saying that I could do anything," his father said. "Groves reminds us all that it's not our personal bomb. It's the Army's. It's something our country has made. We don't have that many A-bombs yet. We haven't built that many. The few we have are very difficult to make. We need to end the war now."

Stephen watched his father lower his eyes to the floor.

"At least now I know why you couldn't tell me the secret," Stephen said. He got up from the bed and moved to his desk and started going through his journal. "You're ashamed of what you're doing." Stephen spoke without looking at his father. "You're going to let them kill thousands of people, and I don't care what you say, many of them *will* be innocent." He could hear Soifer's voice in his mind. See images that had been painted for him. "Dad, you'll be a murderer."

His father turned and started out of the room, but he stopped in the doorway. He came back in and closed the door. He leaned against it.

"Stephen, you think war is something of a . . . well, I think you think it's a game. With your models . . . and your journal. Pictures you cut out of a newspaper. Little notes you jot down. It's more difficult than that, and you've got to understand."

"Well, I don't."

"I don't know when I stopped asking questions," his father said. "I think I used to. I suppose somewhere along the way I decided to quietly do my job. Do as I was told. All of us here. Oppenheimer, and the other physicists. We were all told we could help the war end.

That's why we came here. All we knew in the beginning was that we would save a lot of lives. None of us really thought it through. How could we? We didn't know if we could even make such a bomb. We didn't think how it might be used. We didn't think what it would be like when it was taken out of our hands. Many of us don't like what's happening—"

"Then why don't you stop what's happening, Dad?" Stephen said. "Why don't you do something? Say something?"

His father stiffened and his eyes looked down. "I'm sorry," he said. "Things are the way they are. There's nothing any of us can do about it. I'm also sorry, Stephen, but you're not to leave this house. I don't want you going out until I tell you."

"What? I'm under house arrest for a week? Two weeks?" Stephen looked for weakness in his father's eyes. There was none.

"I'm going over to Alexei's," Stephen said.

"No, you're not," his father said, opening the door. As he started out, Stephen was on his feet. He began to strike out. His fists flew toward the planes and ships, catching in the hanging strings and wings. The models along with his journal fell to the floor. He kicked them and stamped on them, breaking everything. The models shattered. The journal scattered like a pack of playing cards.

His father's hands were on his shoulders.

"Stop it," his father shouted. "Stop!"

But he didn't.

"Stephen, I've got to help you understand," his father said.

"No, you don't," Stephen said. He shook loose, grabbed a shirt, and ran out into the hall-way. A moment later and he was through the living room and out the front door. He heard his father yelling after him. He was running as fast as he could, down the boardwalk and the muddy street—toward the perimeter fence and the west canyon.

18

Stephen ran through the night on the trail that edged the gorge. It didn't matter what lies Sewa or anyone wanted to invent. He had friends he could count on: Alexei and the whole Nagavatsky family. Mr. Nagavatsky, who cared about life and the world and being a father to his son.

The moonlight sliced into the gorge. The railroad bridge with its scattering of red lights was in front of him. Stephen could hear the dogs barking beyond the bridge. There must already be a visitor, Stephen thought, as he climbed the fence of the kennel grounds as a shortcut.

There was a light on in the main house. He saw a station wagon in the shadows of the turn-around. Bright lights spilled out of the slatted windows of the litter shed on the ridge, and shadows played on one of the shaded windows. He was going to call out, to make certain the gating around the shed was secure. *Hey, is that dog tied up? Hey, the dog!*

Maybe there was a new litter—a litter coming now. The fight Stephen had had with his father still made him sick. Puppies. Yes, it would be nice to see puppies. He started up the hill to see if it was Mr. Nagavatsky and Alexei in the shed.

Closer, it seemed he could hear his every footstep—his every breath. Words began to form in his throat, but his tongue was dry, still thick from the shouting.

The front door of the shed had been left ajar, probably for air. Stephen smoothed down the wrinkled front of his shirt and lifted his hair out of his eyes.

Now he could see the glow came from a panel. A console of switches and small lighted dials and what looked like some sort of generator system. Mr. Nagavatsky sat at the console wearing a pair of large earphones and speaking into a mounted radio microphone.

Two large men in suits stood behind him. It took Stephen a while to understand what he was seeing and hearing: a powerful transmitter, with Mr. Nagavatsky broadcasting in Russian.

The litter shed was not a litter shed.

There was motion.

Mr. Nagavatsky took off the headset.

The door of the shed opened wider.

Stephen moved into the shadows against the side of the shed, trying not to breathe. One of the big men walked by and started down the slope. Nagavatsky was in the doorway now, speaking Russian, calling out to the man. But his voice was a mixture of bitterness and anger. A kind of dangerous fury moving in Mr. Nagavatsky that Stephen had not seen before.

There was a growl from the dark shape lying on the floor of the shed. The male dog he'd met once before. With the door wide open it smelled him, Stephen knew. A second later it was on its feet flying toward the door. It would be on him, but a chain snapped it to a halt in midair. The dog spun, twisted, snarling.

Stephen didn't run at first. He walked quickly. Somehow hoping he still wouldn't be seen.

The porch lights of the house came on. The turnaround was lit up. Stephen could see the visitors' car now. A dusty Packard station wagon. Alexei was outside the ranch house with another man.

Stephen was running now, across the grassy slope toward the fence.

"Stephen." He heard Mr. Nagavatsky's voice from the shed. It was the nice voice again. The friendly, resonant voice from the barbecues and the storytelling nights and the Dark Angels. But Stephen knew he had seen something he shouldn't have. The men and the Packard and the lie of the litter shed.

The hidden powerful broadcasting equipment. A chill had seized the back of Stephen's neck. The Nagavatskys *were* spies.

"Wait. Stephen . . ."

Mr. Nagavatsky yelled to one of the men at the station wagon. Mr. Nagavatsky's hands were on the dog's collar, and a second later the dog was loose.

It was a sleek blackness, racing after Stephen. It closed on him faster than he'd thought possible. The fence was too far away for him to make it. Instinctively, Stephen took off his shirt as he ran and threw it behind him. The dog was on it, tearing it, biting it, ripping it to pieces. Stephen leaped for the fence. His hands clamped on the top bar, and his feet dug into the holes between the links.

He heard the dog coming again, but he was over and the dog was left biting the steel of the fence.

The Packard was moving now, turning at the far corner of the kennels. Its headlights were on Stephen as it raced down the dirt road toward the gorge.

Alexei was shouting out the passenger window at him. "Hey, Stephen! Hey!"

The railroad bridge was ahead.

He knew he couldn't go that way—wouldn't go.

The station wagon kept coming. They would catch him. Get him.

There was nowhere *except* the bridge.

The first steps on the ties and gravel were easy. But soon he was over the chasm itself.

He stopped, couldn't move.

The Packard screeched to a halt at the side of the tracks. Alexei got out. One of the suited men had a rifle now. Stephen forced himself to continue across the bridge. He had to look down, advance from tie to tie.

Alexei was on the bridge behind him. The man with the rifle crouched off to the side of the tracks.

Stephen tried to weave.

The shot sounded like a piece of wood splintering.

"NOBODY WANTS TO HURT YOU. IT'S OKAY, STEPHEN."

The man was reloading. This time the bullet was closer, whizzing by his head. Stephen knew he wouldn't make it across the bridge. There was a walkway of planks and steel beams below the track level of the bridge, and he dropped down onto it. Alexei ran until he was above Stephen, then dropped down next to him.

Stephen turned to face him. "Come on," Alexei said. "It's okay."

Stephen backed away from him.

Alexei came closer. "I'm sorry, Stephen," he said, taking out a knife.

Mr. Nagavatsky was with the man and the rifle at the edge of the gorge. He was calling. Shouting directions to Alexei in Russian.

"We're friends," Alexei said softly. "Let's go back, and you won't be hurt."

"No."

Alexei stabbed at the air in front of Stephen. Stephen sidestepped, and the knife blade hit the metal of a beam. Alexei stabbed at Stephen again.

And again.

Stephen turned to run. His feet slipped out from under him. He fell into the bottom web of rods and girders and crossbeams at the middle of the bridge. Alexei climbed down quickly after him. Stephen braced himself against a girder and kicked at the knife. He kicked until the knife fell from Alexei's hands. Alexei grabbed for it but went off balance. He started to fall and grabbed onto one of the beams.

Stephen started to climb back up onto the tracks. Alexei gained footing and climbed up after him.

There was a vibration.

A train was coming.

Close.

Stephen turned to see Mr. Nagavatsky and the man with the rifle silhouetted against the blazing light coming fast around a bend. They ran away from the railroad bed. Alexei was up on the tracks now, running straight for Stephen. He grabbed him and threw him down onto the tracks. Stephen tried to shake him off, to twist loose and get back up.

The train roared onto the straightaway of the bridge. It was traveling fast. Too fast. Stephen heard the roar, felt the metal shaking, shrieking in his ear. Alexei's hand closed tighter on Stephen's neck. His elbow wedged against Stephen's back to pin him down. Alexei's fingers slid under his neck chain, and it broke.

There was a flash. He saw his coin as it fell

toward the river below. He thought of Jackson. And his mother and father, and of dreams that wouldn't come true.

And anger.

He felt the strength of the anger pouring into him.

As the train was bearing down on them, Stephen began to hit back at Alexei.

Somehow Stephen was on his feet again and running. Alexei managed to stand with the train hurtling toward him. Alexei was moving fast, about to catch Stephen again, but another form and clamor rose from the gorge. A huge metal shape with great windows and blinding searchlights.

Stephen could see the face of a pilot through the helicopter's window. A side door was wide open, with soldiers aiming rifles at Alexei.

The train's brakes were locked, its wheels erupting into sparks and fire. Stephen threw himself flat to the side of the tracks and held on to a steel beam above the gorge. He heard the impact as the train hit Alexei. By the time the train stopped, there was a lone shoe lying on a scarlet-red track of the bridge.

Sewa was waiting up when Stephen and his
father were brought home after two in the
morning. The Army's urgent questions had been
asked and answered. Those that hadn't, Dr. Orr
decided, would get dealt with after he and his
son had a night's sleep.

Stephen's bedcovers had been pulled back.
Sewa came in with a hot cup of cocoa topped with
a marshmallow. Stephen took a sip and leaned his
head back onto the white, clean pillows. "I guess
I don't know very much about anything," he said.
"Nothing about picking friends, for sure."

"You'll learn," Sewa said. "You need to live a little longer." She slipped a second marshmallow from the pocket of her apron and placed it in Stephen's cup.

"How did you know so long ago that the Nagavatskys were spies?" Stephen asked. "Weeks. Months ago."

Sewa thought a moment. "I heard it on the radio."

"What?"

"Yes, that was when I first thought it. Russian voices. Stalin. To me, Mr. Nagavatsky sounded like Stalin. A Stalin with red hair. I've always heard cunning in Stalin's voice—when he's on the radio—when he tells us his Russia is our friend. I never believed it. I felt the same about Mr. Nagavatsky. They both sounded false—like liars."

"Alexei too?"

"No," Sewa said. "He just spent too much time looking out your window. At night I could see his shadow fall across the side lawn. Sitting. Watching while you slept. No normal boy likes to watch trucks *that* much."

Sewa smiled. She put her hand on Stephen's forehead to make certain he didn't have a fever from his ordeal. "You're none the worse for wear," she said.

She put out the lights and went to the door. "In the morning we'll talk about friends again. Sometimes true friends are quieter," Sewa said. "They trust that someone they care about very much will finally see the light. Some people come into your life and fade quickly. My father taught me that others come and leave footprints on your heart. Those are your friends."

Stephen sat up on a hill by a children's play fort and looked down on the base. "Hey, you want to play war?" a few of the younger boys asked. "You can attack us. Bomb our fort."

"No, thanks," Stephen said.

"*Hey, you're dead.*"

"*No, I'm not.*"

"*Yes, you are.*"

An M.P. strolled by, patrolling the perimeter fence on the ridge. He watched the kids playing war and then just went on his way. So much for the usual security, Stephen thought.

It was Sunday, and Stephen could see the high school boys playing a baseball game. The cinder-block-and-pipe grandstand was crowded with parents and other kids cheering and eating hot dogs.

The snow at the highest levels of the mountains had melted. The leaves of the cottonwoods had begun to turn brown in the early-August drought. Seen from the hill, Bathtub Row and the rows of houses and Quonset huts looked like part of a board game. The hundreds of Los Alamos telephone poles were crosses rising above the town.

There were several trucks guarded by heavily armed M.P.s at the rear of the Tech Area. Massive custom juggernauts with huge containers and canvas-covered crates chained to oversized flatbeds. There had been no talk of Mr. Nagavatsky or Alexei. No one seemed to notice that they were gone. No one even seemed to notice there were no dogs patrolling the perimeter fences.

His father, in his lab coat, stood with several

of the other physicists. They were sequestered with Oppenheimer away from the main event— the loading of the trucks. General Groves and a cluster of uniformed officers supervised the Special Services men securing the cargo to the flatbeds. Groves never went near the assembly of scientists. He talked only to the drivers and other military men.

Over everything there fell the sounds of cheering from the grandstand.

Stephen knew some of the precious cargo that had been loaded would be on its way to the Lamy train station and the Albuquerque base airport. His father had told him that other larger crates would be transported overland to ships waiting at a dock in California.

When the trucks were ready, Groves and the other officers got into military escort vehicles. The gates of the Tech Area were opened, and the trucks moved out through Security and started the descent down the steep switchbacks.

As Stephen approached the fence of the Tech Area, only his father lingered outside waiting for him.

"Hey, Dad," Stephen called out.

Lately Stephen had begun to accept that his father didn't know all the right words to say, but that he was trying his best. He knew his father wished that he could make all the pieces come together and make sense for him, but Stephen believed they never would.

His father met him at the gate.

"Dad," Stephen said.

"What, son?"

"Remember when we used to walk along the beaches—when you would buy all those shells for me to find?"

His father smiled. "I remember."

"Well, I was thinking about that beach we went to, the one where there were thousands of starfish that were stranded at low tide. Starfish dying, as far as we could see. Seagulls snatching them up, dropping them on the rocks, and eating them. Remember all the starfish in that hot sun?"

"Sure," his father said. "You insisted on taking one of them and throwing it back into the water."

"I remember you telling me that it didn't make any difference," Stephen said.

"Did I say that?"

"Yes."

"I don't remember."

"I do," Stephen said. "Well, I've been thinking about it."

"About that starfish?"

"Yeah. I was thinking that it *did* make a difference. At least to that one starfish."

His father said nothing for a while. "Maybe you're right. . . . I hope so," he said finally, and put his arm around Stephen's shoulder.

"Are we still going to the game?" Stephen asked, brushing his hair out of his eyes.

"Sure," his father said.

They walked across one side of the field to the grandstand, got a couple of sodas, and climbed the steps. They sat at the very top in the bright sunshine. From there they could see the east canyon and the adobe walls of the San Ildefonso Pueblo and—in the distance—the dust rising as the trucks headed off the mesa on their way to end a war.

August 6, 1945
**"Little Boy"
uranium bomb
dropped on Hiroshima—**
140,000 killed

August 9, 1945
**"Fat Man"
plutonium bomb
dropped on Nagasaki—**
70,000 killed

August 10, 1945
**Japan surrenders
without invasion**

A Chronology of Important Events
of World War II and
The Making of the
Atomic Bomb

1939

January 1939

Niels Bohr, a Danish physicist, tells U.S. scientists of a breakthrough: the splitting of the uranium atom (fission), which resulted in a slight loss of mass that was converted into energy. He feels that if a controlled chain reaction can be produced, a huge explosion will result.

August 1939

Albert Einstein writes to President Roosevelt (FDR), stating that a chain reaction has been produced and that further research will lead to the construction of a very powerful atomic weapon. He also warns of Nazi Germany's scientists developing the bomb first and asks FDR to assign someone to lead the U.S. effort to build the bomb.

September 1, 1939

Germany invades Poland. World War II begins. Two days later Britain and France declare war on Germany.

October 21, 1939

FDR appoints uranium committee and tries to secure as many world uranium deposits as possible. Research moves slowly due to lack of awareness of urgency.

1940

Early 1940

It becomes clear that nuclear weapons can cause massive destruction; there is a need for U-235, the uranium isotope that can undergo continuous fission, as the U.S. has a very small quantity.

May 10, 1940

Germany invades Belgium, the Netherlands, and Luxembourg to prepare for an invasion of France. Prime Minister Winston Churchill forms a wartime government in Great Britain.

August 1940–April 1941

Germany attacks Great Britain in the Battle of Britain and London Blitz, air raids prior to planned invasion of Britain.

August 1940

Uranium shipped to New York City, but due to a snafu it sits in storage on Staten Island.

September 27, 1940

Germany, Italy, and Japan form AXIS pact.

1941

Early 1941

Plutonium, an artificially produced radioactive chemical element, is manufactured. Plutonium fissions more powerfully than U-235.

June 22, 1941

Germany attacks Soviet Union.

July 1941

Washington conference report states uranium bomb can be made; work to begin at once.

October 1941

Oppenheimer estimates first bomb can be ready at the end of 1943.

December 7, 1941

Japan bombs Pearl Harbor; Pacific war begins. This is the decisive event that leads to providing funds for accelerated research and production effort on bomb.

1942

Early 1942

University of Chicago chosen as site of first nuclear reactor.

Mid-1942

U.S. begins massive effort to make the bomb, code-named "Manhattan Project."

June 1942

Robert J. Oppenheimer becomes director of group that will design the actual bomb.

September 1942

General Groves of the U.S. Army takes charge of the atomic research project. Site at Los Alamos, New Mexico, chosen. More than 100,000 people and three years will be necessary to complete the project. Acting for the Army, he buys uranium and also site at Oak Ridge, Tennessee, to produce U-235.

December 2, 1942

Crucial experiment: Enrico Fermi tests chain reaction at the University of Chicago and it works: Man can release energy from an atomic nucleus. First man-made self-sustaining nuclear chain reaction achieved.

December 7, 1942

U.S. Army acquires Los Alamos as site of the Manhattan Project.

1943

January 1943

Site acquired at Hanford, Washington, to produce plutonium isotope 239.

Mid-January 1943

Casablanca Conference. At its end FDR announces on the spur of the moment—in front of all—a demand for the unconditional surrender of Germany, Italy, and Japan.

March 3, 1943

Oppenheimer moves to Los Alamos.

April 5, 1943

Scientific staff learn that they will produce a military weapon at Los Alamos.

July 24–25, 1943

Premier of Italy Benito Mussolini resigns and is arrested; a new government is formed in Italy.

August 1943

U.S. and Britain agree to share all knowledge of nuclear weapons, not to use them against each other, not to use them without mutual consent, and not to give any information to a third party.

October 1943

First plutonium shipment arrives at Los Alamos from Hanford.

1944

March 1944

Planning begins for a full-scale test of a nuclear explosion. Oppenheimer names it Trinity—possibly conceiving of the bomb as "the destruction that might redeem."

March 1944

Kenneth T. Bainbridge chosen to find a testing ground in a remote and empty area, with good weather but reachable from Los Alamos. He chooses Jornada del Muerto (Dead Man's Journey).

June 6, 1944

D-Day—Normandy coast of France invaded from the English Channel by the Allies under Eisenhower.

July 20, 1944

Plot by a group of high military and civil German officials to kill Adolf Hitler, Chancellor of Nazi Germany, fails.

September 26, 1944

Largest amount of plutonium 239 ready at Hanford; scientists expect to have a plutonium bomb in the second half of 1945.

Fall 1944

Some B-29s, altered to carry nuclear weapons, arrive on the Mariana Islands, 1,500 miles from Japan; a support base is built at Tinian there.

1945

Early 1945

Oak Ridge begins shipping bomb-grade U-235 to Los Alamos.

March 9, 1945

Allied forces wage massive firebomb attack on Tokyo.

April 1, 1945

U.S. invades the island of Okinawa, establishes air bases 300 miles from Japanese heartland.

April 12, 1945

FDR dies; Harry S Truman becomes president.

April 25, 1945

Truman is informed that in four months the U.S. will have a bomb that can destroy an entire city; he agrees the project is necessary.

April 30, 1945

Hitler commits suicide in Berlin.

May 7, 1945

Germany surrenders; war in Europe is over.

June 18, 1945

Truman approves plan for invasion of main island of Japan.

June 1945

Truman agrees bomb should be used against Japan as soon as possible and with no warning.

July 16, 1945

Trinity—5:29 A.M. First atomic bomb exploded in desert near Alamogordo, New Mexico, 250 miles south of Los Alamos. It is a plutonium bomb with a yield equivalent to 15–20 kilotons (15,000 to 20,000 tons of TNT) and is visible 180 miles away. The Nagasaki bomb will be of this type.

Mid-July 1945

At Potsdam when General Eisenhower is told the bomb is ready to be used against Japan, he opposes it on two grounds: (1) the Japanese are ready to surrender, and (2) he does not want to have the U.S. be the first country to use it.

July 24–26, 1945

Potsdam conference of Soviet leader Joseph Stalin, Truman, and Churchill (replaced in mid conference by newly elected Clement Attlee) calls for Japan's unconditional surrender. Stalin seems unimpressed when told of the new weapon; probably already knew of it. No thought given to use of a demonstration bomb to scare Japanese.

July 28, 1945

Japan seems not to accept an unconditional surrender. Or maybe their reply means they will not comment at present.

July 29, 1945

U.S. cruiser *Indianapolis*, heading back to the U.S. after delivering bomb to the Mariana air base, is torpedoed and sunk by Japanese.

August 2, 1945

Truman gives final okay for use of bomb.

August 4, 1945

Bomber pilot Paul Tibbets and weapons specialist William S. Parsons brief crews on the very destructive weapon they will use. Parsons gives details of the Trinity test. Tibbets is very proud to be part of the raid and thinks it will shorten the war by at least six months.

August 6, 1945

"Little Boy" uranium bomb is dropped on Hiroshima in the morning by a B-29 piloted by Tibbets. The *Enola Gay*, named for his mother, carries a uranium fission weapon yielding an explosion equivalent to about 15 kilotons of TNT. Some 80,000 die instantly, perhaps 140,000 total.

August 9, 1945

"Fat Man" plutonium bomb falls on Nagasaki in the morning, yielding the equivalent of about 20 kilotons of TNT. At least 40,000 die immediately, about 70,000 in all.

August 10, 1945

Emperor Hirohito of Japan, overruling his military leaders, decides to surrender, ending the Pacific war.

August 21, 1945

The bomb's first peacetime death occurs in Los Alamos: A scientist is sprayed by a lethal dose of radioactivity.

September 2, 1945

General MacArthur accepts the formal surrender of Japan in Tokyo Bay on the battleship *Missouri*.

Some of the
Important
People
of the Bomb

Bainbridge, Kenneth T.
Overall director of the Trinity test under Oppenheimer, he investigated and completed all components.

Bohr, Niels
Danish physicist who was a major contributor to the development of quantum physics; served as consultant on the Manhattan Project.

Einstein, Albert
Creative genius and German refugee whose theories revolutionized physics. He did not work at Los Alamos, but his name is connected with the arrival of the Atomic Age.

Eisenhower, General Dwight D.
Commander of the Allied forces in World War II; later 34th President of the United States, 1953–61.

Fermi, Enrico

Winner of the Nobel Prize for splitting the atom, he initiated the first man-made nuclear chain reaction and played a leading role in the Trinity test. He died of cancer in 1954.

Groves, General Leslie R.

Overall military director of the Manhattan Project. He was said to have a large ego (and girth), and he believed in complete secrecy. He was considered insensitive and brusque by various scientists on the project. He had an amazing gift for detail and a love of discipline. Prior to the Manhattan Project, he was in charge of building the Pentagon.

Oppenheimer, J. Robert

Director of the Los Alamos Scientific Laboratory (1942–45). Considered a paradox, he was a philosopher and organizer of the bomb makers. After the war he became a proponent of civilian and international control of atomic energy and strongly opposed the development of the H-bomb on technical and moral grounds. He was suspended by the Atomic Energy Commission in 1953 as an alleged security risk. The case stirred wide controversy, and in 1963 he was awarded the Fermi Prize. He died of throat cancer in 1967.

Parsons, William S.

Directed ordnance (military weapons) division; he was the weapons specialist who armed the "Little Boy" uranium bomb on the way to Hiroshima.

Roosevelt, Franklin D. (FDR)

32nd President of the United States, 1933–45. He died while in office.

Teller, Edward

Physicist; he spent a lot of time studying the theoretical conditions necessary for a fusion (thermonuclear) bomb. After the war he pushed ahead on the super bomb (H-bomb) and became a supporter of big weapons. Called the Father of the H-Bomb, he loved to play Hungarian rhapsodies late at night on his large piano, much to the distress of his neighbors. He was said to be a complex and gifted man who did not work well with others.

Tibbets, Paul

One of the Air Force's best bomber pilots, he flew the *Enola Gay*, which dropped the atomic bomb on Hiroshima. He named his plane after his mother, Enola Gay Tibbets, because she said he would never die flying a plane, when his father rejected his youthful plan to become a pilot.

Truman, Harry S

The commonsense 33rd President of the United States; took office on the death of FDR in 1945 and served until 1953. He made the decision to drop the atomic bomb on Japan.

Sources

Although this is primarily a work of fiction, the following sources were indispensable in writing this story.

Butow, Robert J. C. *Japan's Decision to Surrender*. Stanford, Calif.: Stanford University Press, 1954.

Churchill, Winston. *The Gathering Storm*. Boston: Houghton Mifflin, 1948.

Einstein, Albert, and Leopold Infeld. *The Evolution of Physics*. New York: Simon & Schuster, 1996.

Joliot-Curie, Irene. "Artificial Production of Radioactive Elements." Nobel Lecture, 1935.

Kunetka, James W. *City of Fire: Los Alamos and the Birth of the Atomic Age, 1943–45*. Englewood Cliffs, N.J.: Prentice-Hall, 1976.

Lamont, Lansing. *Day of Trinity*. New York: Atheneum, 1965.

Mason, Katrina R. *Children of Los Alamos: An Oral History of the Town Where the Atomic Age Began*. New York: Twayne, 1995.

Rhodes, Richard. *The Making of the Atomic Bomb*. New York: Simon & Schuster, 1986.

Seddon, Tom. *Atomic Bomb*. New York: Scientific American Books for Young Readers, 1995.

Shapley, Deborah. "Nuclear Weapons History: Japan's Wartime Bomb Projects Revealed." *Science* 199:152–57 (January 1978).

Simpson, Judith. *Native Americans*. Alexandria, Va.: Time-Life Books, 1995.

Sommerville, Donald. *World War II: Day by Day*. Dorset, Conn.: Raintree Steck-Vaughn, 1991.

United States Atomic Energy Commission. *In the Matter of J. Robert Oppenheimer: Transcipt of Hearing Before Personnel Security Board and Texts of Principal Documents and* Letters [1954]. Cambridge, Mass.: MIT Press, 1971.

Zimmerman, Nancy, and Kit Duane, eds. Photography by Kerrick James. *The American Southwest*. Oakland, Calif.: Compass American Guides, 1996.